James Hadley Chase and The Murder Room

›› This title is part of The Murder Room, our series dedicated to making available out-of-print or hard-to-find titles by classic crime writers.

Crime fiction has always held up a mirror to society. The Victorians were fascinated by sensational murder and the emerging science of detection; now we are obsessed with the forensic detail of violent death. And no other genre has so captivated and enthralled readers.

Vast troves of classic crime writing have for a long time been unavailable to all but the most dedicated frequenters of second-hand bookshops. The advent of digital publishing means that we are now able to bring you the backlists of a huge range of titles by classic and contemporary crime writers, some of which have been out of print for decades.

From the genteel amateur private eyes of the Golden Age and the femmes fatales of pulp fiction, to the morally ambiguous hard-boiled detectives of mid twentieth-century America and their descendants who walk our twenty-first century streets, The Murder Room has it all. ››

The Murder Room
Where Criminal Minds Meet

themurderroom.com

James Hadley Chase (1906–1985)

Born René Brabazon Raymond in London, the son of a British colonel in the Indian Army, James Hadley Chase was educated at King's School in Rochester, Kent, and left home at the age of 18. He initially worked in book sales until, inspired by the rise of gangster culture during the Depression and by reading James M. Cain's *The Postman Always Rings Twice*, he wrote his first novel, *No Orchids for Miss Blandish*. Despite the American setting of many of his novels, Chase (like Peter Cheyney, another hugely successful British noir writer) never lived there, writing with the aid of maps and a slang dictionary. He had phenomenal success with the novel, which continued unabated throughout his entire career, spanning 45 years and nearly 90 novels. His work was published in dozens of languages and over thirty titles were adapted for film. He served in the RAF during World War II, where he also edited the RAF Journal. In 1956 he moved to France with his wife and son; they later moved to Switzerland, where Chase lived until his death in 1985.

By James Hadley Chase
(published in The Murder Room)

Consider Yourself Dead

James Hadley Chase

An Orion book

Copyright © Hervey Raymond 1978

The right of James Hadley Chase to be identified as the author of this work has
been asserted in accordance with the Copyright, Designs and Patents Act 1988.

This edition published by
The Orion Publishing Group Ltd
Orion House
5 Upper St Martin's Lane
London WC2H 9EA

An Hachette UK company
A CIP catalogue record for this book is available from the British Library

ISBN 978 1 4719 0399 1

www.orionbooks.co.uk

One

Frost got talking to a high class hooker in a dimly lit, chromium plated bar off Broadway. She explained she was waiting for a client who was generally late as he had a wife problem. Frost told her he was just waiting. She was blonde and very chic with a traffic stopping body. Making chit-chat, she said she was going to Paradise City at the end of the month.

'That's where the real action is,' she said, her blue-grey eyes sparkling. 'There's more money to be picked up there than in any other city in the world.'

There were two things that interested Frost, apart from women: money, and then more money. He said he had never heard of Paradise City. What was so good about it?

She was one of those girls, given an audience, who never stopped talking. This, of course, Frost thought, didn't make her unique. He could say that of all the girls he knew and had known.

'Whereas Miami is known as the millionaire's playground,' she told him as if reading from a guide book, 'Paradise City is known as the billionaire's playground. The extra naughts make all the difference.' She closed her eyes and made yum-yum noises. 'Paradise City is around thirty miles south of Miami. It is super de luxe where anyone with what it takes, can pick up a load of the green stuff.' She leaned back and looked searchingly at Frost. 'Now a stag like you could have a real ball there.'

She went on to explain that fifteen per cent of the City's population represented the stinking rich. Fifty per cent

1

represented the various well paid serfs who kept the stinking rich in luxury. Thirty per cent were the workers who kept the City ticking over, and five per cent were the girls and the boys who latched on to the stinking rich and, if they were smart enough, picked up enough folding money to keep them happy until the following season when they descended once again on the City.

As Frost was urgently looking for money, he expressed interest.

Again she regarded him. If he hadn't been sure that she would cost him the whole of his payroll to haul her into bed, he would have taken a very serious interest in her, but he knew a doll of her class was way out of his money bracket.

'What's your line?' she asked.

'The same as yours – the fast buck.'

'Apart from your looks, what's your talent?'

Frost frowned. What was his talent? This was something he hadn't thought about before. He was now thirty-two years of age. For the past twelve years he had scratched up a living, always on the look out for the big money, but up to now, never finding it. Right now he was unemployed. He was in New York, hoping to find an opportunity that paid well without too much sweat.

'Security,' he said. 'Using my muscles. The last job I had was riding a truck as a guard. I goosed the old man's secretary, and got the gate.' He grinned at her. 'Right now, I'm looking for something.'

'With your looks and build,' she said, 'you could get yourself a rich old woman in Paradise City who would pour bread into your lap.'

Frost grimaced. He said rich old women weren't his thing.

She flicked her fingers at the waiter and ordered another dry martini. Frost still nursed his Scotch, but he did make motions of reaching for his wallet when her drink came, but she shook her head.

'I run an account here.' She accepted the cigarette he

offered, then said, 'If you really are after the fast buck, here's what you do. Go to Paradise City. Contact Joe Solomon. You'll find him in the book. He handles all us folk who are after the fast buck. Tell him you are a friend of mine, and I'll hate him if he doesn't fix something for you. I'm Marcia Goolden.' She looked across the barroom and heaved a sigh. 'Here's my freak. Call Joe.' She gave Frost a sexy smile. 'See you in Paradise City. You and I could have fun together. Joe'll tell you where to find me.' She finished her drink at a gulp, slid off her stool and walked over to a fat, balding man who was staring around like a fugitive from a chain gang. She hooked her arm in his and led him out into the hot, humid sunshine.

Frost had been in New York for five days. He had been offered a job here and there, but the money didn't interest him. He thought about what Marcia had said. Why not? he thought. What have I to lose except the airplane fare?

Frost believed in conserving his money. When he had booked into the Hilton hotel, he had with him a shabby suitcase containing the bare necessities and his oldest suit. His best clothes in a good suitcase he had left in the left-luggage depot at the airport. He spent one more night at the Hilton, then leaving his oldies to take care of the check, he took a flight to Paradise City with his better possessions.

From Marcia's description, Frost was prepared for the City, but when he came out of the airport, he found himself gaping. Every car, waiting to pick up passengers, was either a Rolls, a Bentley, a Caddy or a Benz. He asked the cabby to take him to a cheap hotel.

The cabby stared at him as he picked his gold teeth with a gold tooth pick.

'There ain't such an animal, bud,' he said. 'The cheapest is the Sea Motel. It costs thirty a day, but I wouldn't put my old mother there.'

Frost said the cabby's mother could be more fussy than

he was, and if that's the cheapest the cabby could suggest, he was prepared to try it.

Frost had one thousand dollars saved, but as he was driven through the City, he felt his money shrinking. Sky-scrapers, luxe hotels, the fantastic beach with sun umbrellas, shading well nourished, brown bodies, the vast stores, the luxe boutiques, the moving crowd, all looking a million dollars, made, to Frost, an alarming picture of wealth, but once through the City, the scene changed.

The cabby explained this was the district where the workers lived. The small villas, the seedy-looking walk-up apartment blocks and the weather-beaten clapboard cabins made a sharp contrast to the gold-paved sidewalks of the City.

The Sea Motel was hidden away, as if ashamed of itself, up a cul-de-sac. Twenty cabins, all in need of paint, built in a semi-circle around a plot of yellowing grass restored Frost's confidence and swelled the money in his wallet.

The recepion clerk, ageing, sun-bleached, gave Frost a welcome. He said he had a nice cabin at forty a day. This cabin had a tiny bedroom, a small living, shower and toilet. In the living-room there was a sagging armchair, a settee with grease marks, a table, two upright chairs, a TV set that would have delighted an antique dealer, and a thread-bare carpet, pitted with cigarette burns. The view from the window gave on to dusty palms and a row of over-flowing trash bins.

Frost haggled for ten minutes and finally got the rate down to thirty a day. With a dismal expression, the reception clerk said there was a snack bar across the way.

As soon as he had taken himself off, Frost looked up Joe Solomon in the book. He found the number and called.

A cool female voice said, 'This is the Solomon Agency.' She made it sound as if she were announcing the White House was on the line.

'I want to talk to Mr Solomon,' Frost said, and swatted at a fly that was crawling up his sleeve. He missed the fly that came back to crawl over his hand, sneering at him.

'Who is this, please?' Her voice sounded bored as if she had asked the question a million times.

'Mr Solomon wouldn't know me. I'm looking for a job.'

'Please write in and state your credentials,' and the line went dead.

Frost stared into space. He felt lonely, although he had the fly for company. He was playing this all wrong, he told himself. This was Big Time. Unless you were Small Time, you didn't talk to a snooty chick who was paid to give the brush off, you talked to the Boss. After thought, he went over to the reception cabin.

The ageing clerk was propping himself up on the counter, staring at nothing. Two flies were taking their morning constitutional walk over his bald head. He paid them no attention.

'Can I borrow a typewriter for a couple of hours?' Frost asked.

The reception clerk stared at him as if he had just landed from the moon.

'What was that again?'

Frost pointed to the battered looking typewriter on the desk behind the reception clerk who looked around, stared at the typewriter as if he hadn't seen it before.

'Can I borrow that?' Frost produced a dollar bill.

The reception clerk eyed the bill, let the two flies play tag in what was left of his hair, then nodded.

'Help yourself.'

'Got any paper?'

The reception clerk thought about this, then reluctantly heaved himself to the desk and produced some sheets.

Frost gave him the dollar and lugged the typewriter back to his cabin. He spent a sweaty hour typing. When he returned the typewriter, the clerk was still in the same position, but another fly had joined the other two.

The book had told Frost that Joe Solomon had an office on Roosevelt boulevard.

'Where do I find Roosevelt boulevard?'

'City centre: runs parallel with Paradise boulevard.'

'How far from here?'

The reception clerk pulled at his nose, thought, then said, 'Give or take, five miles.'

'Have you a car I can rent?'

'Five bucks a day. That one over there in the last bay,' and he pointed.

The car was a beaten up VW. Frost decided anything was better than walking five miles in this heat. The car got him to Roosevelt boulevard without falling to bits.

Joe Solomon's office was on the tenth floor of an impressive high rise with four express elevators, air conditioning, and important looking people moving around the vast lobby with that busy, preoccupied air of ants on the march.

A Spanish-looking chick sat behind a desk in Solomon's outer office. Her long black hair lay on her shoulders and made a frame for a face that had everything until you reached her eyes. They were black, and they had seen everything, and what they had seen, they hated. Her age would be around thirty, but she had already lived eighty years of experience, and each year had increased her hate. Frost thought she was a very tough cookie.

She looked him over. He was wearing his best suit: light cream with a faint, narrow blue stripe, a dark blue shirt and a white tie. He had checked himself on the fly blown mirror at the cabin before leaving. He thought he looked pretty impressive, but he saw at once his size, his looks and his clothes made as much impact on her as a lump of dough thrown against a brick wall.

He decided to play this one brisk.

'Mr Solomon,' he said.

Black eyebrows lifted.

'You have an appointment? Your name?'

'The name's Frost. I have something better than an appointment,' and Frost dropped the letter he had written, sealed in an envelope, on her desk.

She regarded the envelope as she might regard something nasty the cat had brought in.

'If you will give me your telephone number, Mr Frost, you will be contacted.'

He placed his big hands on her desk and leaned towards her. She gave off a faint body smell that if bottled would have been a rave as an after-shave lotion.

'I know J.S. likes to play hard to get,' he said, smiling at her. 'I know you are paid to sit where you are sitting, making it easy for him to feel important. It's all part of the racket, but I don't buy it. J.S. is here to make money. I can make money for him. Suppose you get off your fanny, give him this letter, and if he doesn't want to talk to me, I'll let you spit in my right eye.'

Her eyes widened, then she laughed, and when she laughed, she really looked a beauty.

'I thought I'd seen them all,' she said, 'but although the dialogue is corny, at least, it's a new approach.' She picked up the envelope and stood up. She had a sensational body. 'It won't buy you anything, but you deserve a try.'

She went through a doorway behind her desk, swinging her hips. At least that was a step forward, Frost thought as he looked around. For an outer office it was very lush. The nigger brown carpet, the apricot coloured walls, the picture window with a view of the sea, the battery of telephones, the built-in filing cabinets and the three lounging chairs along the far wall produced an air of considerable prosperity.

He thought of the letter he had written:

Dear J.S.
Marcia Goolden told me to look you up. She said if you played the Big Shot with me she would hate you for the rest of your life.
Do you care?

Mike Frost.

He wondered if he should get out his handkerchief to wipe his right eye when she came out. Maybe Marcia had been playing at being important. Maybe Solomon would come out and spit in his left eye, but he needn't have worried.

The chick came out, smiling, and jerked her head.

'He'll see you. It still won't buy you anything.'

Frost leered at her.

'Want to bet?' and he walked past her into a vast room that was more a lounge than an office. Apart from a big desk by the picture window, the rest of the room resembled a millionaire's nest where he can entertain some fifty people without feeling crowded.

Behind the desk which was big enough to play billiards on, sat a fat little man in a grey suit that must have set him back seven or eight hundred dollars. His round, sun baked face, with hooded eyes, a nose like a buzzard's beak and a mouth like a pencil line was framed with long white hair down to his collar.

He watched Frost cross the big room, then he smiled and waved Frost to a chair.

'Very nice, Mr Frost. How's Marcia?'

'Fine and busy,' Frost said, sitting down.

Solomon nodded approvingly.

'There's a worker!' He leaned back in his executive chair. 'She's my favourite hooker. There's not much I wouldn't do for Marcia. I take it you're here for a vacation and employment to defray expenses?'

'Right,' Frost said.

'You've come to the right place. What's your line? What are you looking for?'

Frost produced the details of his various qualifications he had typed out, and handed them over.

'This covers my working life, Mr Solomon. Maybe you can get ideas from this how to fix something for me.'

Solomon read what Frost had written, whistling softly from time to time.

'You seem to have had a number of jobs in the past twelve years,' he said, laying down the paper. 'Let me see, three years as a patrolman with the New York police, promoted to Detective, second grade, resigned after two years to join the F.B.I. as field agent. Resigned after three years to become a rifle man in Vietnam. You then became a bomb instructor for the I.R.A. You later became a mercenary in the Angola upheaval. Finally, this year you worked for a short time as a security guard for Western Security Corp in Boston.' He cocked his head on one side. 'Quite a life of action and violence.' He picked up the paper again and read on: 'Knowledge of most modern weapons and explosives, judo black belt, karate, marksman with military citations, pilot's licence etc. etc.' He put down the paper. 'Very impressive, Mr Frost, but no one is planning to start a war in Paradise City. I feel your talents would be wasted here.' He brooded, then went on, 'There are jobs, of course, I can offer you, but . . . '

'Such as?'

'With your looks and build, you could earn five hundred a week. I have an old trout who needs a chauffeur, but you would have to lay her regularly once a week.'

'Not my thing,' Frost said firmly.

'I didn't think it would be. I have a very rich queer who needs a companion, but you . . . no, I can't see you filling that bill.'

'Nor can I.'

'How would you like to be a life-guard? It pays around a hundred, but it's as good as a free vacation. All you have to do is sit on the beach and wait for someone to drown.'

This suggestion appealed to Frost until he considered the salary.

'It has to be a lot better than that. From what Marcia told me, I'm expecting to pick up big money.'

Solomon sighed.

'That old trout . . . '

'That's out. How about a bodyguard?'

Solomon brightened. He leaned forward and thumbed a buzzer. The Spanish chick looked in.

'Any vacancies for a bodyguard, Carmen?'

'Not right now.' She gave Frost a jeering smile. 'Strictly

a drug on the market,' and she removed herself, shutting the door.

'From time to time, we do get requests for a body-guard,' Solomon said. 'It's your best bet. Suppose you hang around? If I hear of something . . . '

'I can't afford to hang around,' he said. 'Okay, if that's all you can do, I'll call Marcia. Maybe she can do some-thing for me while she's hating you.'

Solomon winced.

'Don't do anything hasty. Give me a couple of days . . . okay? I'll get Carmen to go through our files. Give her your telephone number. We'll find you something.'

'Two days, then I call Marcia.'

Frost left him and went into the outer office.

Carmen smiled jeeringly at him.

'I warned you. Give me your number, but don't squeal if you don't hear from us.'

Frost wrote down the telephone number of the Sea Motel and laid it on her desk.

'Get me a good job, baby, and I'll buy you a ribbon for your typewriter,' he said.

'More corny dialogue,' she said, and reached for the telephone.

Back in his sweltering cabin, Frost settled down to wait. If Solomon didn't come up with something, Frost knew he was in trouble. He had no idea how to contact Marcia, and even if he did contact her, he didn't think she could help him. He had just to wait and hope. So that was what he did – hoped and waited. Scared to leave the telephone, he sent over to the quick-snack bar at lunch time for a sandwich and beer. The beer was flat and scarcely cold, the sandwich could have been made of cotton wool.

At 20.00, Frost decided Solomon and the Spanish chick had gone to their respective homes, and it would be safe to take a swim. He spent until midnight, swimming, lazing under the palm trees, and watching the dolls and their boys having a ball. He felt lonely.

He slept late, had luke warm coffee that should have been ashamed of itself, then dressing, he sat down to wait again.

By 15.00, after another gruesome lunch, he was fit to be tied. Maybe, he told himself, it hadn't been such a hot idea to come to this City. He was now sorry he had listened to Marcia's sales talk. Then just when he was deciding to cut his losses and take a look at Miami to see if there was anything cooking there, the telephone bell rang.

It was Solomon on the line.

'I have a job for you, Mr Frost. Will you come to my office immediately. It's a matter of urgency.'

'The knock you are hearing on your door is me arriving,' Frost said, hung up, bolted to the VW and was on his way.

* * *

The Spanish chick was at her desk manicuring her nails when Frost hurried into the outer office.

She gave him a stony stare and flicked her fingers at Solomon's office door.

'There you are, Mr Frost,' Solomon said, from behind his desk. 'Sit down. A job's come in that's custom made for you.'

Frost sat down.

'What's it pay?' he asked.

'Six hundred a week, your own quarters, all found. Nice, huh?'

Frost said it was nice.

'You know the Agency's terms?'

Frost cocked an eye at him.

'Not yet, but you're sure to tell me.'

Solomon chuckled.

'Fifty per cent of your first week's salary and ten per cent until the job folds.'

'No wonder you can afford to wear a suit like that,'

11

Frost said. 'Well, okay. What's the job?'

'Bodyguard. That's what you want, isn't it?'

'Whose body do I guard?'

'Mr Grandi is a very valuable client of mine. He has reason to be anxious about his daughter's safe keeping. He has a permanent home in Rome. An abortive, but vicious attempt was made to kidnap the girl while in Rome. Mr Grandi, naturally alarmed, has rented a villa on Paradise Largo where he has installed his daughter. He thinks, away from Rome, she will be safe.'

'Grandi? Who's he?'

Solomon made an impatient gesture.

'Carlo Grandi is the richest industrialist in Italy. Rumour has it he is worth several billion dollars. He is, as I have said, one of my most valued clients. I have supplied all the staff at the villa, and I arrange everything for his daughter's comfort.'

'Several billion dollars?' Frost's ears pricked up. 'What's the daughter like?'

'I haven't had the fortune to meet her nor Mr Grandi. I deal through Mr Grandi's major-domo, Mr Frenzi Amando.' Solomon grimaced. 'Now, there is a difficult man, but that's neither here nor there. The reason why I have had this urgent request for a second bodyguard is that Mr Amando, checking during the night, found the night guard asleep. He was instantly dismissed.' He paused to light a cigar. 'I have highly recommended you, and Mr Amando is prepared to give you a month's trial. He relies on me to check out references and so on, and I have told him your background is impeccable.' He looked slyly at Frost. 'It is, isn't it?'

'You can say that again,' Frost said, with a grin. He now understood why the Agency's terms came so high.

'I didn't mention your more violent activities, Mr Frost. I feel that would be unwise. I told him you have been a detective attached to the N.Y.P.D., then a Federal Agent, and recently a security guard. He seemed satisfied.'

'You mean the job's mine?'

'Yes, if you want it. I have several applicants for body-guards, but as Marcia is a friend of mine and yours . . . ' He waved his cigar in the air.

'I want it. So what do I do?'

'You are to report to Jack Marvin who is the senior guard. He is expecting you. Mr Amando may not find time to see you himself. He's a busy man, but if he does see you, watch your step.' He pushed a slip of paper across his desk. 'Here are instructions how to reach the villa. Paradise Largo is where the very wealthy live. Villa Orchid – Mr Grandi's residence – is on an island. Access to the Largo estate is over a bridge which is constantly guarded. You will have to show your driving licence to the guard who has been alerted to expect you. I suggest you pack, and get over there pronto. Okay?'

Frost got to his feet.

'I'm on my way, and thanks.'

Solomon waved that away.

'Anything for Marcia.'

'Where does she stay when she's here?' Frost asked as he moved to the door.

Solomon eyed him.

'Didn't she tell you?'

'I forgot to ask.'

'The Spanish Bay hotel – where else?'

'Is that something?'

'The best and the most expensive. Marcia can pick up a thousand bucks a night when she's in the mood.' He rubbed his hands. 'What a worker!'

Going into the outer office, Frost saw Carmen had finished her repair work on her nails and was now reading a legal looking document.

'The job's mine,' Frost said, pausing at her desk. 'I owe you a ribbon for your typewriter.'

'Shove the corn,' she said curtly, 'and sign this.' She handed him the document. 'It's your contract with this agency.'

Frost took a chair near her and read the document carefully. He read the small print even more carefully. All money due to him in wages were paid direct to the agency. Having made commission deductions, what was left was to be paid into an account in his name with the National Florida Bank. He was insured for ten thousand dollars against accident, the premium deducted from his earnings. If he didn't hold the job for more than two weeks, there would be a further deduction of fifty per cent on the last week's salary.

'You certainly know how to look after yourselves,' he said taking the pen she offered and signing.

She didn't bother to answer that one.

'How about a little celebration dinner tonight?' he said, without much hope. 'I could show you my press cuttings, and you could show me yours.'

She gave him a stony stare.

'Piss off,' she said, and reached for the telephone.

You can't win all the time, Frost thought as he took the elevator to the ground floor, but, at least, you can try.

* * *

Paradise Largo turned out to be an isthmus linking E.1 to A.1.A. highways, halfway between Paradise City and Fort Lauderdale.

The causeway to the estate was guarded by a lodge and an electronically controlled barrier.

A big hunk of beef, in a bottle green uniform, a .45 colt on his hip, surveyed the VW as Frost pulled up before the barrier. He then surveyed Frost who could see from the expression on the guard's face, he didn't think anything of the car nor of him.

Taking his time, the guard came out of the lodge and took Frost's driving licence.

'Jack Marvin's expecting me,' Frost said. 'Mr Grandi's place.'

The guard read everything, including the small print on the licence, then handed it back.

'Second on the right and straight ahead to the next guard house,' he growled, then went back into the lodge.

Frost took the second on the right and drove down a broad avenue, newly sanded. On either side were ten feet high hedges. Every now and then, the hedges were broken by high, oak nail studded gates, leading to some villa. To Frost, the smell of wealth was overpowering.

At the end of the road, he came to another guard-house. The barrier was up and another hunk of beef was waiting.

'Straight ahead,' he said, staring at the VW as if he couldn't believe his eyes. 'Park in bay 10. Marvin's there, waiting for you.'

Frost drove over a fifty yard long bridge, spanning the sea water canal. Ahead of him he could see an island in the middle of the lagoon. The island was screened by closely planted mango trees. Over the bridge, he saw ahead, ten foot high double gates. They swung open as he reached the far end of the bridge. As he drove on to a broad sandy drive, he saw, behind the screen of mango trees a ten foot high fence of electrified wire. In his driving mirror, he saw the double gates had already swung shut.

A hundred yard drive through a forest of papaya and loquat trees brought him to Grandi's residence.

The villa was two-storey, Spanish style, covered with red and white bougainvillaea. The villa probably had some fifteen bedrooms. To Frost, it looked enormous. In the front of the villa was half an acre of lawn and a small lake with a playing fountain. Beds of roses and begonias made splashes of colour.

Near the villa was the car park. A cream and brown Rolls Camargue sneered at a sky blue Lamborghini that, in its turn, sneered at a silver Benz.

As Frost parked the VW in bay 10, a tall, thin man, wearing a grey suit, dark blue slacks tucked into Mexican boots, came out of the shade and advanced towards him.

On his hip was a .38 police special. He wore an Australian style hat, the sides laced up.

As Frost got out of the car, the thin man joined him. Steady, steel grey eyes set in a thin, hard face, surveyed Frost, then he thrust out his hand.

'Jack Marvin.'

Frost shook hands.

'Mike Frost.'

'Suppose we walk around, and I'll wise you up on the job?' Marvin said. 'The first thing you'll want is a uniform like mine. I'll tell you where to get it. I've already talked to the cops, and all you have to do is to go to the cop house for a gun permit. We have an armoury here, and you can take your pick. As you'll be on duty at 20.00 tonight, there's a bit of a hustle.' He moved into the shade and led Frost down a narrow path, bordered by orchid trees, talking as he went. 'This is an easy job. The security is more or less taken care of by electronics, but all the same, you have to be constantly on the alert. In the guardroom in the villa there is an alarm panel and TV scanners. Your job is to watch the alarm panel and the scanners, and keep watching. It's a hell of a boring chore. I guess you spotted the electrified fence as you came in. Don't go near it. It's lethal. If some smart ass, using insulated cutters, opens a way in, an alarm alerts the cop house and shows on the panel in the guardroom. The island is completely enclosed by the fence. We don't reckon to have trouble during the day. There are too many boats on the lagoon, and as you've seen, the entrance is well guarded. At 21.00, four Doberman Pinschers have the run of the island. They are killers: make no mistake about that. When on night shift, you stay in the guardroom. Don't go out unless you want your throat torn out. The dogs know me. I let them out and lock them up when I come on duty during the day.' They came out of the shade, and into the open by the fence at the back of the island. Frost could see the sea water canal ahead. Already there were a number of motor cruisers and yachts roaming aimlessly. The crews were either fat old men and their fatter wives or lean young men with their dolls. The scene reeked of wealth. 'Just along here,' Marvin said, 'is where the boats are kept.' He moved on and reached a gate, overlooking a harbour in which floated a sixty-foot motor yacht, a Cris-craft and a dinghy with an outboard motor. Marvin waved to the boats. 'All so much waste of money. No one uses them, but they are there, if anyone wants to.' He spat at the fence. 'I guess all these rich punks on the estate have boats, so we have boats too.'

Leaving the harbour, he led Frost towards the villa. Frost was absorbing the scene, missing nothing. Finally, they came to the villa, and Marvin led Frost along a broad sandy lane until they paused before an oak, nail studded door.

'This leads to the guardroom,' Marvin said, producing a key. He unlocked the door and Frost followed him into a large, air-conditioned room. There was a battery of TV sets against a wall. By them was a big panel covered with red, yellow and green lamps. On another wall was a gun rack. The arsenal was impressive: two shotguns, two automatic rifles, a tear gas exploder and a range of hand guns. A table and two chairs occupied the centre of the room. Two lounging chairs stood before the TV sets.

'Here's where you work nights,' Marvin said, closing the door. 'You sit in one of those chairs and watch the panel and the monitors. You keep awake. Joe went to sleep, and Old Creepy caught him. If you want to stay with this job, you don't go to sleep. You have the night shift this week, I take it next week.' He went to a big closet, opened it to reveal a refrigerator. From it he took two cans of beer, gave one can to Frost and waved him to a chair.

Frost sat down, saluted Marvin and drank.

'Old Creepy? Frenzi Amando? Solomon mentioned him.'

Marvin nodded and sat down.

'Right. The original sonofabitch. I like this job. The bread's fine. The conditions are good. Wait until you see your living quarters: very, very nice. I've been here now for three months, but old Creepy spoils the scene. There have been times when I've nearly banged his rat teeth through the back of his neck. He looks for trouble. The sonofabitch loves trouble. He loves waving his power.' Marvin drank from the can. 'So if you want to keep this job, and it's worth keeping, watch it with Amando.'

'Solomon said there was a snatch threat,' Frost said. 'Right?'

'That's the reason for this operation.' Marvin took a pack of cigarettes from his shirt pocket and offered it. They lit up. 'I'll put you in the photo. Grandi – he's the boss – has lots of dollars. Just to give you an idea, if he lost five million, it would be the same as you losing twenty cents, and I'm not kidding. Five months ago, when he was in Rome, an attempt was made to kidnap his daughter. Let me tell you about her. She's young, something to look at, spoilt, a bit of a hellion, and until this kidnap attempt, had the run of Rome. Grandi is besotted with her. The kidnap attempt scared the crap out of him. It ended with four thugs getting killed and two cops died later. Grandi decided to get his daughter out of Italy. He rented this place, fixed the security and the daughter now lives here.' Marvin grimaced. 'I'm sorry for her. She is virtually a prisoner. She never leaves the island. She has swimming in the pool, two new movies a week, and TV, but that is a hell of a bore after living wild in Rome. Grandi visits her every six weeks. Old Creepy makes sure she remains on the island, and makes sure you and I do our job.' He looked at Frost. 'Got the photo?'

Frost waved to the TV monitors and the panel.

'So all I have to do is sit tight here and watch? Suppose the red comes up?'

Marvin pointed to a door.

'That leads into the living quarters of the villa. You don't use it unless the red goes up. If it does, you grab an automatic rifle and go to the bottom of the stairs, leading to the sleeping quarters. You stay right there so no one gets up to Gina's room – that's the daughter. When the red light goes up, the cophouse is alerted, and within a couple of minutes, the cops arrive.'

'And the dogs tear them apart.'

'The dogs are well trained. If they haven't already fixed any intruder, then another red light goes up. There is an electronically controlled whistle that only the dogs can hear, and when they hear it, they go back to their compound and the gate automatically shuts. Give or take, five minutes, you'll have the cops in your lap, and I'll be around too.'

'Sounds as if I'm going to earn my bread the easy way.'

'Sounds like it, doesn't it? The trick is always to be alert so Old Creepy doesn't stick a knife into you, and don't kid yourself it's easy to stay alert through a long, dull night.'

Frost shrugged.

'I've had worse jobs. Talking about jobs, did Joe Solomon fix you here?'

Marvin shook his head.

'I don't give ten per cent of what I earn to a smart shyster. I was a State trooper for fifteen years. My wife and I fell out.' He took a drink and grimaced. 'I guess we got married too young. On my own, I found it was no fun being a cop in a rented bungalow. I got talking to Tom Lepski, a good friend of mine. He's a first grade detective at the cophouse. He told me about Grandi needing a bodyguard. I sold myself to Old Creepy and got the job, and I fixed Joe Davis, a buddy of mine, to be second guard. I earn eight hundred a week. I have a cabin to live in with a Jap to take care of me. All meals – and good ones – are provided.' He grinned. 'As long as it lasts, it's the best.'

Frost mentally noted that Marvin didn't belong to the 'fast buck' people. They finished their beers, then Marvin got to his feet.

'I'll show you your cabin.'

Frost followed him around the back of the villa, past a vast swimming pool, equipped with lounging chairs and a bar where a small Japanese, in a white coat, was rinsing glasses. He eyed Frost, then bowed to him.

'That's Suka. He looks after us,' Marvin said, without stopping. He went down a narrow path. They hadn't gone far before they heard the savage, spine-chilling sound of barking dogs.

Around a bend in the lane, they came upon a wired-in compound where four enormous Doberman Pinschers stood in a threatening row, barking and snarling.

'Wrap up!' Marvin shouted at them, and the dogs immediately became silent, their eyes on Frost.

'Keep clear of them,' Marvin said. 'They are killers.'

Frost believed him.

Passing the compound, they came on two wooden cabins.

'This is yours. The one next is mine.'

Marvin pushed open a door, and they entered a big living-room, comfortably furnished, plus a TV set and a stereo radio, then through to a big bedroom, a well-equipped bathroom and kitchenette.

'Nice, huh?'

Frost looked around. It was more than nice: it was luxe.

'Just one thing to remember,' Marvin said, his expression serious. 'No women here, even if you could smuggle a woman in which you can't.'

Frost nodded, thinking what a hell of a waste of a luxe cabin.

'I hear you,' he said.

'When you are on day shift, which will be next week, you clock off at 20.00, then your time's your own, but you must be back here by 02.00, that's danger time, but be back before, in case Old Creepy checks.'

'How about transport?'

'There's a T.R.7 in the garage. We share it.'

'So I drive back late and get chewed up by the dogs.'

Marvin grinned.

'No problem. You keep the car windows closed and drive straight into the garage. The door is electronically controlled. Maybe the dogs will bark around the car, but they have been trained not to enter the garage. When the door shuts, you get out, and there's a door from the garage into your cabin.'

'Quite a setup.'

'I guess.' Marvin shoved his hat to the back of his head. 'Well, Mike, you'd better get your uniform, and then go to the cophouse for your pistol permit. Harris on Trueman avenue will fit you out. He knows what you'll want. Get back here around 19.00. We'll have dinner together in the guardroom. You won't complain about the food. You take what comes, but it's always good. I guess that's it. I'll get back on the job. See you,' and nodding, he left.

Frost drove the VW to the outfitters and came away with three sets of uniform and an Australian style hat. Then he went to the policehouse and picked up his pistol permit, then he drove to the Sea Motel, settled his check, got a taxi and was driven back to the Grandi estate.

He felt relaxed and happy. He thought of Marcia. She had done him a good turn. At six hundred a week and all found, on the face of it, the job appeared to be a beautiful steal.

Long may it last, he thought as the taxi took him towards Paradise Largo. Man! Am I on the gravy train!

Gravy train?

He was to find out later how wrong he could be.

Tough as he was, money conscious as he was, if he could have looked into a crystal ball and seen what was coming, he would have got the hell out of Paradise City on the first available plane.

Two

Frost looked at his strap watch. The time was 01.15. He yawned, rubbed his eyes, and yawned again. He should have gone to bed early the previous night, he told himself, instead of lying on the beach until midnight. He had another seven hours before Marvin relieved him. It had been a mistake to have eaten that excellent, but heavy meal of beef fillet cut in fine slices and done in some rich sauce. Maybe he shouldn't have drunk three bottles of beer.

The four colour TV monitors had a soporific effect. The pictures kept changing, showing various parts of the island, mostly dense foliage. A couple of times, he caught sight of a dog, but the rest was green and trees. He felt his head fall forward and he jerked himself upright.

If you want to keep this job, don't go to sleep.

Well, he had been warned. Making an effort, he got to his feet and began to walk around the room. He told himself he had better not sit down again, but grimaced at the thought of pacing up and down for the next seven hours.

He paused and took in several deep breaths of the air-conditioned air. Then crossing over to the conditioner, he turned it fully on. The sudden blast of cold air cleared his head. He stood before the machine, breathing deeply, then with enough cold air in his lungs, he became alert.

Leaving the machine at maximum, he walked over to the gun rack and took down one of the automatic rifles. He checked the magazine. The rifle was ready for instant

22

use. As he was balancing the weapon in his big hands, his sensitive ears, long trained in jungle fighting, picked up a faint sound.

He looked across the room at the door leading into the villa. He saw the door handle was turning.

Now fully alert, he moved swiftly and silently to one of the big lounging chairs, dropped on one knee, the rifle aimed at the door, his body half concealed by the chair.

The door edged open without sound.

'Stay right where you are or you'll get lead in your gut,' Frost snarled in his cop voice.

There was a pause, then a voice said, 'This is Mr Amando.'

Frost grinned. Old Creepy had nearly caught him napping!

'Push the door open and stay where you are,' he snapped.

The door swung fully open. Standing in the doorway was a thin man of medium height, wearing a white tuxedo, a blood red bow tie and midnight-blue trousers.

Frenzi Amando was nudging fifty years of age. He had a skull-like face, topped by thick sable-coloured hair. His parchment-like skin was tight over symmetrical features: high forehead, deepset black eyes, a long, pinched nose, an almost lipless mouth and an aggressive chin. Frost told himself he had never seen a more menacing character: something right out of a horror film.

Slowly, Frost lowered the rifle and stood up. If he wanted to keep this job, he reminded himself, he had to play the right cards.

'Sorry about that, sir,' he said. 'But may I suggest you don't creep up on me? I'm here to protect you and Miss Grandi.'

Amando regarded him for a long moment. His eyes reminded Frost of the eyes of a cobra: flat, glittering and deadly. Then he moved into the room.

'You are Frost?' The voice was soft with a hissing note.

'Yes, sir.'

'You appear to be alert. That is what you are paid to be. In the future, you will not be so dramatic. Only I use this door, and no one else. Do you understand?'

Frost laid the rifle across the arms of the chair.

'I react to sound, sir,' he said. 'I've been trained that way. I will remember in the future if you wish to check on me, I won't shoot.'

'I found the last guard asleep.'

'Then you have every right, sir, to check on me.'

Amando stared at Frost, his glittering black eyes suspicious.

'You have been well recommended. This, of course, is your first guard duty.' The thin lips curved into a sneering smile. 'New brooms, as they say. Keep alert, Frost. From time to time, I will check, as I check on Marvin,' and turning he left the room, shutting the door silently.

Frost blew out his cheeks. If this sonofabitch had crept in three minutes earlier, he would have caught him, napping. Picking up the rifle, he returned it to the rack. He was now fully awake.

So that was Old Creepy. He could now understand why Marvin had said Old Creepy spoilt the scene.

He lit a cigarette, dropped into the lounging chair and looked at the monitors. He watched a dog cock his leg against a tree.

He thought of the six nights ahead, sitting in this chair, staring at the monitors, not knowing if the door behind him would silently open, and he grimaced. Maybe he was not going to earn six hundred a week, and all found, as easily as he had thought.

After a while, he began to think of Marcia Goolden. He saw her again as she sat by his side in the dimly lit bar: blonde, grey-blue eyes, beautiful. *See you in Paradise City. You and I could have fun together.*

Had she meant it?

He got a hard on as his mind dwelt on her. He looked at his strap watch. The time was now 01.20.

She would be a night-bird.

There was a telephone book on a shelf. It took him only a minute or so to find the number of the Spanish Bay hotel.

'Give me reception,' he said, when he had made contact.

After a moment's delay, a smooth, quiet voice said, 'Can I help you?'

'Has Miss Goolden checked in yet?' Frost asked.

'Yes, sir.'

'Put me through.'

A pause, then the smooth quiet voice said, 'Who is this, please?'

Frost hesitated. Would she remember him? He thought for a brief moment, then thinking, What have I to lose? he said, 'Mike Frost.'

'Will you hold a moment, Mr Frost? Miss Goolden may have retired.'

Frost waited, aware he was breathing heavily, aware his hand, holding the telephone receiver, was clammy.

Then her low, sensual voice came on the line.

'Hi, honey! So you arrived!'

Frost drew in a long, deep breath. From experience, he knew he had the green light.

'Hi, baby! I've had you on my mind ever since we parted.'

She laughed.

'I bet! Did you see Joe?'

'I saw him. I'm home and dry, thanks to you. When do I see you, baby?'

'Joe fixed something for you?'

'He sure did. When do I see you to say thank you?'

She laughed.

'How do you say thank you, Mike?'

'Wait and see. Just give me the chance to see you. When?'

'Man! You sound impatient! She laughed again. 'I'm impatient too. Come here tomorrow at twelve midday. You know the time, you crazy man? I'm going to bed.'

'I'll share that bed with you in your dreams.'

She laughed and hung up.

Frost slowly replaced the telephone receiver. The prospects for tomorrow looked good.

He settled down in the lounging chair, lit a cigarette, and waited impatiently for the moment when Marvin walked in to relieve him.

* * *

The doorman of the Spanish Bay hotel, a coloured giant, resplendent in a pale blue tunic, white trousers and a black top hat, advanced with dignity as Frost slowed the T.R.7 to a standstill.

The doorman lifted his hat and regarded Frost with an inquiring lift of black eyebrows.

'Shall I take the car, sir?' he asked.

Then Frost saw Marcia Goolden coming down the hotel steps.

'Just picking up a fare,' he said, and got out of the car as Marcia joined him.

She looked sensational, Frost thought. She was wearing white slacks and a skimpy red halter that scarcely contained her heavy breasts. Her corn-coloured hair fell in silky waves around her deeply tanned shoulders.

'Hi, Mike!' she exclaimed as the doorman lifted his hat and bowed to her. 'I'll drive,' and before Frost could stop her, she slid into the driving seat. 'We're going to a dump that's not easy to find,' she went on as Frost settled into the bucket seat beside her. She sent the car shooting down the hotel drive, braked as she reached the boulevard, then forced the car into the traffic. 'This is terrific!' she said. 'I'm thrilled Joe has fixed you.'

'Not without your influence.'

Marcia laughed.

'You had trouble with that Spanish bitch? I'm not surprised.' She weaved the car through the traffic, and once or twice Frost flinched. They escaped two collisions by the margin of a coat of paint. She waved gaily to the stunned-looking drivers as she sped on. 'She's Joe's screw, but he's so busy making money, she doesn't get enough.' She whipped the car off the highway and went storming along a dusty dirt road that abruptly opened on to a wide stretch of tarmac, fronting a long two-storey building, very lush, with dark blue and gold sun awnings. On the roof ran the legend: The Ace of Spades. There were tables dotted around under sun umbrellas, and immaculately dressed waiters in red coats, serving drinks. 'This is my work shop,' she said as she swung the car into a parking bay. 'We can eat well here, then you can say thank you,' and she regarded him with merry, laughing eyes.

As she led him into the restaurant, a fat, smiling Maitre d', bowed to her. His black eyes ran over Frost, then he gave him a little bow. With his right hand held high, he conducted them along the aisle between the tables. As Frost followed Marcia's swinging hips, he glanced round. This was some joint, he thought. In the centre of the vast room there was a playing fountain, the cascade of water kept changing colours. In the big pool, containing the fountain, was a tiny island on which stood a grand piano. A thickset, coloured man played immaculate swing: gently and softly. Frost regarded the people at the tables: fat, thin, all bronzed, all in sun dress: women in bikinis or halters and slacks: the men, hairy chested, in shorts. Some of them raised languid hands, some holding fat cigars, as Marcia progressed towards a table away from the pool. She waved, twitched her hips, and reaching the table, she sat down in a blue and gold armchair. Frost, slightly dazed by the opulence of the room, dropped into a chair at her side.

The Maitre d' flicked his fingers and the wine waiter appeared.

What the hell is this going to cost me? Frost thought uneasily and mentally fingered his billfold.

'Gin or whisky?' Marcia asked him.

'Whatever you have,' Frost said.

'Martini gin,' Marcia said, smiling at the wine waiter. 'The usual, Freddy.'

The wine waiter bowed and went away.

'Relax, honey,' Marcia said, laying a cool hand on Frost's wrist. 'I own this dump. Everything is for free.'

Frost gaped at her.

'You own this place? You must be kidding!'

She giggled.

'Fact . . . it's a story. Let's eat. I'm starving.' She patted his wrist. 'Let me order, honey. I check the menu every day. Okay?'

'Go ahead. You really mean . . .'

The Maitre d' moved forward.

'Gaston, we'll have the prawn salad with the trimmings, the duck in that tricky brandy and cherry sauce and coffee.' She looked at Frost. 'Sounds right? You can have anything else if you don't like duck.'

'Sounds fine.'

The Maitre d' went away.

'You really mean you own this place?' Frost said, staring around.

She nodded, sipped her martini, then sat back.

'It's a story, honey. Three years ago, I worked Miami. I had a pad on the second floor in a quiet side street. I was doing all right, making around two grand a week. One night, a guy propositioned me.' She laughed. 'This guy was really kinky. He said he would be outside my complex every Sunday morning at nine o'clock. All he wanted me to do was to show myself at the window and wave him away. That's all he wanted. For that, he left five hundred bucks in my mail box. The longer I kept him waiting before I waved him away, the better he liked it. This went on for eighteen months. It used to half kill me, dragging myself out of bed at nine in the morning, but the bread was sweet. Then one day, he wasn't there. You know, after all that time, I missed the freak. Then his attorney wrote, telling me his client had died and had left me this joint. Now can you believe that?'

'You mean this freak actually left you this setup in his will?'

Marcia nodded.

'That's what he did.'

Looking around the lush restaurant, envy gnawed at Frost.

'There are times when I wish I'd been born a woman!'

Marcia laughed.

The prawns were served, and they began eating.

'You . . . born a woman? Don't kid yourself, honey. To be a successful career girl, you have to take a lot. Girls always get the shitty end of the stick.' She grimaced. 'Okay, I've been lucky, but I've earned my luck. I'm twenty-five. In another five years, I plan to retire. I own this place. I'm learning to run it. Then . . . ' She paused to heave a sigh. 'No more freaks. No more filthy old men. No more being scared of a sick with a knife.' She looked at him, her eyes serious. 'Don't ever wish you were born a girl.'

Frost thought about this, but he wasn't convinced. To own a lush joint like this! Again envy gnawed at him.

'Now tell me about your job,' Marcia said.

Six hundred a week! he thought, and this hooker must earn thousands! He ate. The big prawns were succulent, but envy had dried his mouth.

The wine waiter poured a chilled Chablis, then moved away.

'Well, it's not much,' Frost said. 'I got myself a job guarding a wop's daughter.'

'A wop? Who?'

'Carlo Grandi. He's supposed to be a big shot in Italy. He's scared his daugher will be snatched.'

'Carlo Grandi?' Her voice shot up a note. 'A big shot? Honey! He *is* Italy's Big Shot. You really mean Joe's fixed you to work for Grandi?'

'Yeah, but what's so hot about that? Okay, Grandi has quite a place and he seems loaded, but the job's only worth six hundred a week.'

Marcia conveyed a prawn to her mouth.

'You have yourself a job, honey!'

'You think so? Six a week? You must be making thousands.'

She regarded him thoughtfully.

'What so wrong about six hundred a week?'

'I've got ambitions.' He continued to eat. Then after a pause, he went on, 'I want to live like these slobs,' and he waved a hand to take in the whole of the restaurant. 'I want real money, not a crappy six hundred a week.'

'Who doesn't?' She finished the prawn salad and leaned back in her chair. 'But, honey, use your head. You have your foot in the door. You've started right. Tell me about the job. What do you do?'

Frost told her. He was still telling her when the duck was served.

'Have you met Grandi's daughter?' Marcia asked as they began to eat.

'Not yet. Marvin tells me she has hot pants.' Frost grinned. 'That's something I could take care of for her.'

'Not with Amando around.'

Startled, Frost stared at her.

'You know about him?'

'Honey, I know everyone around here. It's my business. I have a date with that creep every first Saturday of the month.' Marcia pulled a face. 'There's a cold fish: strictly an in and out job: nothing fancy: just letting off steam, but he pays.'

'He's right out of a horror film.'

'You can say that again.' She smiled at him. 'How about Marvin, the other guard? Do you jell with him?'

Frost shrugged.

'I wouldn't know yet. It's early days. From what I've seen of him he is a dedicated cop: a guy without ambition.' He ate, then said, 'This duck is fantastic.'

'All the food here is fantastic.' She paused to look directly at him. 'Honey, you shouldn't gripe. Sitting in a chair, just watching, getting well fed and well paid, isn't something to gripe about, is it?'

'I've got big ideas. I look around. You, and everyone around here, are loaded. Grandi! A goddam wop! It kills me to think a wop could have so much money.'

'He worked for it, honey. I worked for what I've got. What you put in, you take out. If you want real money, begin to think what you can put in.'

Frost scowled.

'You sound just like my jerk of a father. He was always yakking about putting in and taking out. He put in, sweating his stupid guts out fourteen hours a day, but he never took out.' Frost clenched his fists as he thought back into the past. 'My father! Now there was the original pea brain! Don't feed me this crap about putting in and taking out. That's strictly for the birds!'

The waiter came and removed the plates. Frost sat back and looked around the lush room. This was his scene! This must be his future background if he could only find the key to the fast buck. His mind floated around his ambitions: to own a villa like Grandi's, to own a big motor cruiser, a Lamborghini, to snap his fingers to have a doll drop on her back, and to have big money to spend.

The coffee was served.

Frost was so wrapped up in his futile dream of wealth that he wasn't aware that Marcia was studying him searchingly.

'A nickel for your thoughts,' she said.

Frost smiled crookedly.

'This joint! All these slobs with money. What I wouldn't do to be one of them!'

'I told you, honey: this is the city of the fast buck,' Marcia said. 'You've only just arrived. Be patient.' She pushed back her chair. 'I have a call to make,' and before he could get to his feet, she was already walking away, waving to people who waved languidly back.

The wine waiter appeared.

'A cognac, sir?'

31

'Go peddle your swill some place else,' Frost snarled. He felt so frustrated he had the urge to get away from this lush room with all these stinking rich around him, but he restrained himself. He had come here for one purpose: to get this blonde, sensational woman on a bed.

He was finishing his coffee when Marcia joined him.

'Let's go now and look at my etchings,' she said, and looking up, Frost saw the hot desire in her grey-green eyes.

As he pushed back his chair, feeling a wave of lust run through him, he wasn't to know the intimate corner table at which they had sat was bugged and every word of their conversation was now on tape.

* * *

Their explosive union was over.

Frost lay on the king size bed, staring up at his reflection in the mirror that covered the ceiling. This was an angle of his body he had never seen before, and he felt a male pride in his muscles, his tanned lean body, the length of his legs and his handsomeness. In the past, he had had countless women, but, apart from a coloured air hostess who he still remembered with awe, he couldn't recall any other woman being so technically expert and as satisfying as Marcia.

She was, of course, a pro. She knew all the tricks, but unless he was kidding himself, he thought he had really turned her on. But had he? Being cynical, and always suspicious of women, he reminded himself she just might have been putting on an act.

He listened to the sound of the shower in the bathroom across the room, then he looked at his strap watch. The time was 16.15. He still had some hours before he reported for another night's stint at the Grandi villa.

Propping himself up on his elbow, he looked around the big room that was immediately above the restaurant. He thought the room must be soundproofed as he heard no sound from below. To his right was a big window that overlooked the swimming pool and the colourful garden. Marcia had told him the window was of one-way glass. He could stand naked before it, looking out, and no one below could see him.

The big room reeked of wealth. The white lamb's-wool carpet, the almost silent air conditioner, the mirrors, wall-to-wall, and on the ceiling, the elaborate cocktail bar, the soft swing music coming from concealed speakers, and the rest of the trappings created a de luxe nest for men who could afford to pay the money Frost longed to have.

Marcia came from the bathroom. She was naked. Frost felt a little catch at his throat. She was really something to look at, he thought, and lust stirred in him as he sat up and swung his feet to the carpet.

'Honey, you must go now,' Marcia said, slipping into frilly panties. 'I have to get back to work.'

'Okay.' Frost stood up.

She was now in slacks and a T-shirt. As she ran a comb through her silky blonde hair, she said, 'Go down to the pool, Mike. I want you to have a ball here.' She smiled at him. 'I'm going to see a lot of you, honey.' She reached in her handbag, then taking out what looked like a credit card, she came over to him. 'Take this, honey.'

Frost took the card and regarded it suspiciously.

'What's this?'

'You flash it around honey, and everything here is for free. It's a member's card, only you don't get a check.'

'What the hell does that mean?' Frost demanded aggressively. 'I pay my way,' but he held on to the card, staring at it, seeing his name printed on it.

'It's a tax deductible gimmick,' Marcia explained. 'You're not the only one. How else do you imagine we can run a place on this scale? Take it, and don't get on your high horse. I do something for you, you do something for me,' and her hand went down on his crotch for a brief moment, then she moved away, smiling at him.

Frost grinned at her. He again stared at the card.

'You really mean this card takes care of the check?'

'That's what I said. Get dressed, Mike, and get the hell out of here!' There was now a snap in her voice. 'Go down and have a ball. I've got work to do!'

'Yeah . . . sure.' He scrambled into his clothes. 'You mean I can go down there and act like one of those slobs?'

She laughed.

'That's what I mean. See you tomorrow. We'll have a repeat performance. Same time at the Spanish Bay. Okay?'

Frost grabbed her and kissed her.

'You bet it's okay.'

He walked down the stairs, leading to the vast terrace and the pool, clutching the credit card she had given him.

Marcia watched him go, then she shut the door and turned the key. She leaned against the door and drew in a long, deep breath.

One of the narrow mirrors on the wall, facing her, suddenly slid aside, and a man moved into the room. This man was Marcia's uncle: the only man she really feared. His name was Lu Silk. By profession he was a killer, hiring himself out to the highest bidder. Providing you had the right introduction, and you were rich enough, anyone who was putting pressure on you, was being a continual nuisance, who was fooling around with your wife or your girl friend was quickly dead after you contacted Silk. Silk was a professional. His killings never came back to him.

He had a sinister appearance: hatchet-faced, with a glass right eye and a white scar running down his left cheek. It was the glass eye that terrified Marcia. When he spoke to her, she found herself staring with horror at the glass eye and never at his live one.

Silk was around forty-six years of age, tall, thin and dressed in a white shirt and black slacks. His grey-black hair was slightly receding. Around his sinewy left wrist was a heavy gold bracelet: around his right wrist was a black-faced quartz watch.

For the past two years, Silk had worked exclusively for

Herman Radnitz who was perhaps the most evil and powerful force behind the world's political scene. Silk was on a retaining salary of four thousand dollars a month. At a moment's notice, he had to make himself available to wipe out a nuisance who was bothering Radnitz. When the killing had been expertly accomplished, a large sum of money was paid into Silk's Swiss banking account. This arrangement had suited Silk well enough, but for the past two months, he had been idle. Radnitz was in Pekin, and was then moving to Delhi. He had told Silk to take a vacation.

This vacation of unknown duration worried Silk. He was a high spender, and a compulsive, unlucky gambler. For some time now, he had been thinking of ways and means to break away from Radnitz. He was getting the impression that Radnitz was going to use his killing talents less and less. It was time, Silk told himself, to make provision for his future.

He had an arrangement with Marcia that, when she entertained a client for lunch or dinner, a tape recording of the conversation should be made available to him. Over the past week the various conversations he had listened to had given him food for thought. Several possibilities had alerted his active mind: a chance for blackmail, a chance to make a quick profit on the stock market, a chance for extortion, but, after thought, he had decided the risk involved didn't justify the gain. Sooner or later, he told himself, something important would turn up. He aimed for the Big One that would put him on the gravy train for the rest of his days: nothing but the Big One would satisfy him.

When listening to the conversation between Marcia and Frost, he thumped his fist into his palm. Here, at last, he thought, could be the Big One.

Ever since Carlo Grandi had rented the island villa on Paradise Largo, Silk, knowing this villa had been rented as a sanctuary for Grandi's daughter, had considered the possibilities of kidnapping the girl. The ransom, he knew, would be enormous. He was sure Grandi would pay at least twenty million dollars to get his daughter back.

Urged on by the thought of owning so many millions, Silk had discussed the possibilities with two men who worked with him, and who were also on Radnitz's payroll.

These two men, Mitch Goble and Ross Umney, were experts at setting up an operation. Silk had told them to take a long look at Grandi's place, and to estimate the chances of snatching the girl.

After a few days, they came to Silk and told him to forget the idea. No one, they said, was going to snatch Grandi's daughter, not, at least, as the present setup stood. They explained about the security of the island, the dogs, and particularly about Marvin.

'If this fink could be approached,' Goble said, 'there's a good chance, but no way. Marvin can't be bought. I've gone into his background in depth. He's one hundred per cent straight ex-cop, and no one, repeat no one, will bend him. No dice, Lu, skip the idea.'

So regretfully, Silk had put the idea out of his mind. When Goble said there was no way, he meant just that. Silk had learned to trust Goble's judgement. A couple of times in the past he had brushed Goble's advice aside, and each time, he had nearly run into disaster. Now, he knew better.

So okay, he thought regretfully, Grandi's daughter stays safe.

But listening to the conversation between Marcia and Frost, he realised that the chance to pick up around twenty million dollars was no longer a pipe dream.

When Marcia had excused herself to Frost to make a telephone call, she had contacted Silk. He had told her to give Frost the V.I.P. treatment.

'Sink your hooks into this guy,' Silk had said. 'I need him.'

As Silk moved into the room, Marcia gave him a scared, hesitant smile.

'Was it okay?' she asked.

'Okay, so far,' Silk said. 'Get this into your head, chick, we need this guy, so keep him hot. I'll handle the rest of the scene. Your job is to keep him hot.'

Marcia nodded. When Silk gave instructions, she always obeyed.

'You're a smart chick,' Silk said as he sat on the arm of a chair. 'You're asking yourself why we need this guy. I'll spell it out to you. In a few months this joint is going to fold. You don't understand figures, but I do. Your overheads are far too high. That black boy playing the piano is fine, but he eats your profits. Your wage bill is also eating into your profits. I looked at your balance sheet for last month. You're already in the red. Did you look at it?'

'Charlie showed it to me. I thought next month . . .'

'There could be no next month. Do you want to keep this joint?'

Marcia's eyes opened wide.

'Keep it? It's my future!'

'What it now needs is a big shot in the arm, and Frost can give it, and he can give it to me too, so keep him hot.'

'How can he? He's worth nothing.'

'You keep him hot. I'll handle the rest of the scene.' He stared at her, his glass eye glittering in the sunlight, then he reached for the telephone.

'Give me Mr Umney,' he told the operator on the club switchboard.

'Yes, sir.'

He waited.

Then Umney came on the line.

'Hi, there, Lu!'

Silk began to talk.

* * *

'Hi, there, Mr Frost!'

Frost, who had been standing in the shade, watching the clients disporting themselves in the vast swimming pool, looked around.

37

A heavily built, jovial looking man had come up to him. His fleshy face, with a wide, friendly smile, exuded charm. Tall, muscular, around thirty-six years of age, dark and sun-tanned, wearing only white slacks, Ross Umney conveyed a bonhomie that was slightly overpowering.

It was said of Umney, and with reason, that he could charm a rat out of its hole, a lollypop from a child, a big chunk of money from a shrewd business man, and even the platinum dental plate from a dowager.

Umney was considered by the Paradise City's criminal fraternity as the best con man in the game. Behind his jovial, smiling face and his charm lurked a ruthless, vicious mind intent only on conning some sucker out of his/her money.

Silk, who was top of his profession as a hired killer, regarded Umney as a big asset. Without Umney to set up an operation, Silk's various assignments would have been next to impossible.

Umney had a remarkable ability to finger closely guarded, near inaccessible men whom Radnitz wanted out of the way. Umney was able to gather essential data without creating suspicion, and this data he passed on to Mitch Goble who was Silk's technical expert. Goble in his turn, would assess the data, then pass judgement. If he gave the green light, Silk would then, and only then, move into action.

Umney had been relaxing in his air conditioned room, above the kitchens of the restaurant, when Silk's telephone call came through. He listened to what Silk had to say, then said, 'Can do – will do,' and he went in search of Frost. Finding him, Umney switched on his charm.

'Hi, there, Mr Frost!'

As he offered his hand, Umney regarded Frost, thinking: 'This cookie is no push over. Softly, softly. He will need handling.'

Puzzled, and a little suspicious, Frost shook the extended hand.

'I'm Ross Umney,' Umney went on, exuding charm.

38

'I'm the official host around here. My job is to keep every-one happy. Marcia told me to take care of you . . . this is my pleasure. You know something, Mr Frost?' He paused and beamed, then went on, 'Or may I call you Mike?'

Still suspicious, but relaxing to Umney's charm, Frost nodded.

'Fine . . . Mike. As I was saying, when Marcia gives one of her special friends the V.I.P. treatment, I give him the V.I.P. treatment or else . . . ' He laughed. 'That's my job. What can I do for you? You name it, you'll get it. How about a swim in the pool? There's a boutique here to fit you out. Do you want company? We have a load of hostesses. They are all willing, and you can take your pick. Would you dig our massage parlour? We have two Jap babes who really know their business. We have a movie here. You say the word, and I can fix it for a private show. Our movies are so hot we have to use an asbestos screen.' He laughed. 'Maybe you like fishing? We have a trout pool. Maybe you like golf? We have a driving range. We have a car shuttle service down to the sea. Maybe you'd like to take one of our babes for a fast ride in a speedboat? Water ski-ing? Skin diving? You name it, Mike, you get it.'

While Frost was staring at this smiling, jovial man, un-able to believe that he was being offered all these trap-pings of the rich, a short, fat man came up.

'How about my boat, Ross?' he demanded, a peevish frown on his face. 'You said you'd fix it.'

'Hi, there, Mr Bernstein. It's all fixed. Did you ask at the desk?'

'Didn't know I had to. Where the hell is the car?'

Umney pointed.

'The green Caddy, Mr Bernstein. Joe's waiting . . . no problem.'

The fat man grunted and walked off.

Umney sighed, smiling at Frost.

'That's Bernstein. He's worth millions. You know, Mike, this is a hell of a job. None of these rich creeps is ever satisfied. Now . . . you . . . what can I fix for you?'

None of the suggestions Umney had offered appealed to Frost. Some other time, he might give the massage parlour a twirl. He had heard of Jap girls, but Marcia had so drained him, any form of exercise was strictly out.

'Nothing right now, Ross,' he said. 'Thanks all the same. I guess I'll get moving . . . some other time, huh?'

Umney looked alarmed.

'Hey! You can't walk out on us, Mike! Marcia would have my balls.' He laughed. 'Are you interested in shooting?'

Frost regarded him.

'That's one thing I'm tops at . . . why?'

'Excuse me for asking, but are you really good?'

'That's what I said. Why?'

'We have a guy here who thinks he's a male Annie Oakley,' Umney said. 'He drives me nuts. He's offering a thousand bucks to anyone who can outshoot him with a .38 at twenty yards. I can't find any takers. Do you think you could take a grand off him?'

Frost hesitated. He had been the best shot with a handgun and a rifle while in the Army, but that had been sometime ago. A thousand bucks?

'Who's this guy?'

'A club member. He practically lives in the shooting range. I could fix up a match right now. If you're as good as you say, it'd be an easy way of picking up a grand.'

'And an easy way of losing it,' Frost said cautiously. 'What age guy is he?'

'He's an oldie . . . around fifty, and he has only one eye.'

'Fifty and one eye?' Frost grinned. 'Sure, I'll take him on.'

'Here's what we do, Mike. We wouldn't want you to lose a grand. You'll be doing us a favour by taking him on. You beat him and the grand is yours. He beats you and we pick up the tab . . . what do you say?'

Frost grinned again.

'What have I to lose?'

'Let's go down to the range. He'll be there right now.'

They found Lu Silk in the well equipped basement shooting range, talking to Moses, the coloured attendant, who kept the range clean, changed the targets and acted as scorer when there was a shooting match on. There were no other sportsmen. Silk had had the range closed to other clients. He wanted Frost on his own.

Umney made introductions, and Silk offered what seemed a flabby hand which Frost shook.

Among Silk's many talents was the ability to convey the impression that he was a little feeble, and edging into premature senility. Frost regarded him searchingly, and was completely taken in by Silk's act. He decided this was going to be a push-over, and, he began to wonder what he would do with the thousand dollars he was going to pick up.

Umney was saying, 'Mike's a good shot, Mr Silk. He would like a match.'

Silk nodded, then looking at Frost, he said, 'Have you got a thousand, sonny? I don't take on a match with a piker.'

Frost bristled.

'Are you calling me a piker?' he snarled, his face flushing.

Silk appeared to shrink a little.

'Forget it . . . just so long as you have the money.'

'I've got the money,' Frost snapped, 'and another thing . . . don't call me "sonny", or I'll start calling you grandpa . . . right?'

Umney said hastily, 'Now, gentlemen . . .'

Silk retreated a step.

'Sure . . . sure, Mr Frost. Forget it . . . suppose we start shooting?'

Moses came over with a long leather case containing six .38 police specials.

'Take your pick, Mr Frost,' Silk said. 'I have my own gun.'

Frost took his time. He examined each of the six guns.

Finally he selected one of them that sat well in his hand.

Moses ambled down the range and set up two targets.

'We toss for the first shot . . . best out of five,' Silk said, and promptly won the toss. This suited Frost. He wanted to judge just how good this one eyed fink thought he was.

Silk took up his position. Watching, Frost decided he had an old fashioned stance. His feet were spread wide and he extended his shooting arm, the gun pointing like a finger. His left hand hung by his side. Strictly for the birds, Frost thought.

The gun exploded into sound.

Moses peered, then pressing a button signalled 'Outer 25'.

Silk muttered under his breath and then stepped aside. Grinning, Frost swung up his gun, holding it in both hands, right leg forward, a perfect balance. He fired.

Moses signalled 'Inner 50.'

Should have been a bull, Frost thought. The gun throws to the left.

Silk fired.

'Inner 50.'

Frost aimed a trifle to the right.

'Bull 100.'

They shot three more times. Silk failed to score a bull. Frost scored a bull, an outer and an inner.

Moses computed the scores. Frost 340. Silk 225.

His hatchet face expressionless, Silk took out his wallet and produced two five hundred dollar bills.

'You're quite a shot, Mr Frost,' he said, then as he was about to give the bills to Frost, he paused. 'Suppose we try again? Five thousand evens. Give us both an incentive, huh?'

Frost hesitated.

Silk went on, 'I'm getting an old man. I need a leak. I'll be right back,' and he walked away to the toilets.

Frost grinned. This was taking a dummy out of a baby's mouth. Now he had the feel of the gun, he was sure there would be no problem.

Umney said, 'Don't risk it, Mike. You've won your grand. Forget it.'

'This guy isn't with the scene,' Frost said. 'Of course, I'll take him.'

'Look Mike, you'll be on your own. If he beats you, I can't ask Marcia to finance you for five grand. Forget it.'

'I can't lose, Ross. I've already taken a grand off him. I'd be out of my mind not to take five more off him. I've got this fink taped.'

'Okay,' Umney said. 'You have a point.'

Somewhere in the range, a telephone bell rang. Moses ambled away, and while Umney was lighting a cigarette, Moses called, 'You're wanted upstairs, boss. Mr Seigler . . .'

'I'll be right back,' Umney said. 'Good shooting.'

As he hurried to the elevator, Silk came from the toilets.

'Well, Mr Frost, do we have a match?'

Frost nodded.

'Five evens?'

'Sure.'

'Sure.'

While they were talking, Moses was cleaning the guns and loading them.

'Where did you learn to shoot?' Silk asked.

'The Army.'

'Fine training.' He accepted his gun from Moses. 'You have the first honour. Suppose you have your five shots? I'll follow you . . . right?'

'Sure.' Frost took the gun, balanced it in his hand and waited for Moses to put up two new targets. When he got the green light, he steadied himself. Five thousand! A dummy from a baby! He took his time, aimed fired, aimed fired, paused, then fired three more times. Then he stood back. He heard Moses whistle, then the figures came up on the board: 452.

Beat that, you old fink, Frost thought. The five thousand was as good as in his pocket.

Silk wandered up, the gun slack in his hand.

'Damn good shooting, Mr Frost. Well . . . let's see what grandpa can do.' Suddenly, his thin body seemed to come alive, his feet spread, his arm came up and five shots hammered out: bang-bang-bang-bang-bang!

Frost gaped. This old fink must be out of his mind! He hadn't even taken aim. He wouldn't be even near the target at that speed.

Then as figures appeared on the board he saw 500, a chill ran down his spine.

'Let Mr Frost see my target,' Silk said.

Moses came running up, grinning and thrust the target into Frost's hand. The bull had been completely cut away. He stood staring at the target. He had been conned! He had fallen for one of the oldest tricks in the world, and he was in the hole for four thousand dollars!

'That's shooting too, Mr Frost,' Silk said with a wintery smile. 'No immediate rush. I'll keep the grand I owe you and you give a cheque to Mr Umney for four thousand. He'll give it to me.' He walked over to the elevator, leaving Frost alone with Moses who continued to grin.

'That Mr Silk sure is a big conner, boss,' he said. 'He sure makes a lot of bread down here.'

Frost stared sightlessly at the negro, then dropping the target, he walked slowly over to the elevator and stood waiting until the engaged signal flashed off.

Three

Catching the last rays of the sun, Gina Grandi lay on a lounging chair, and stared across the big, lonely swimming pool.

She was wearing an emerald green bikini which went well with her Venetian red hair. Her heart shaped face was expressionless. Her body, heavily sun tanned, was well proportioned: her breasts a little heavy, her hips rounded and solid, her legs long and slim.

She spent most of her days thinking back into the past when she had been the toast of Rome's *Dolce Vita*. Because of this stupid kidnap attempt, she was confined behind an electrified fence, and she had no idea when her father would relent.

How she hated her father!

For the thousandth time she thought of that disastrous night when she was getting into her Lamborghini, and four men had suddenly surrounded her, guns in hands.

She had been dining at one of the fashionable cellar clubs with a party she had found boring. She had excused herself, leaving them half drunk and shouting. As she was unlocking her car, these four men appeared out of the darkness. They were all young, thin, dressed in shabby jeans and leather jackets. They were all bearded and, to her, excitingly dirty looking.

She immediately realised they intended to kidnap her. The realisation sent a sensual wave through her body. To get away from the boredom of luxury, to be hidden in some sleazy apartment, to be raped even, was something she had realised, with a slight sense of shock, she had been subconsciously yearning to happen.

But how stupid and incompetent these four had been! They had been waiting outside the club, all hoping for millions, but without a plan in their retarded minds. Their furtive movements had attracted the attention of two alert policemen who had taken cover behind a car and had watched them.

Kidnapping in Italy was rife, and every policeman had been instructed to watch for any suspicious action.

As the four young men surrounded Gina, she had smiled at them, unafraid of the guns in their hands. Her heart began to pound with excitement.

'Come with us,' the tallest of the four had said. 'This is a snatch!'

Then out of the darkness, a voice barked, 'Police! Drop those guns!'

The tall youth, who could not have been more than eighteen years of age, swung around and fired.

The policeman who had moved out from behind the car was hit, but before dropping, he shot the youth, killing him.

There was an immediate panic among the other three. They turned to run. The other policeman, shielding himself behind the car, his gun hand on the roof of the car, picked off two of the youths as they ran. The fourth youth, short, thickset, had dodged behind the Lamborghini. He caught sight of the policeman's head. Standing up, he fired as the policeman fired. Both shots were killers.

Gina had stood motionless during the gun battle. She was still standing, staring at the six bodies as her friends spilled out of the club and press photographers appeared from nowhere. While standing amidst the screams, popping flashlights and seeping blood, she had a sick feeling that something very special in her life had been snatched away from her.

The publicity had been world wide. Every newspaper carried a front page photograph of her, surrounded by bodies. The snide papers had underlined that she had just left a club which had an unsavoury reputation: the haunt of gay men, reefer smokers and kinky women.

When her father heard what had happened and had read the reports in the papers, he took instant action.

Carlo Grandi was a ruthless tycoon who had fought his way up from a Naples slum to being the richest man in Italy. He spent every hour of his waking life controlling his vast financial kingdom. His wife, bored and lonely, scarcely ever seeing her husband, had had an affair with a playboy whom she had met at a party, given by one of her women friends. The playboy had tried to blackmail her. Terrified of her husband, sick of her empty, rich life and sick of herself, she drank a bottle of vodka, swallowed sleeping pills and died. Grandi returning from a business trip, found her with a sad little note that read: *Forgive me, Carlo. Your standards were too high.* The suicide had been hushed up. Gina, then seventeen years of age, was at a Swiss finishing school. She had a cable from her father which read: *Mother died. Heart attack. Coming to see you.*

Grandi arrived at the Montreux school. Gina had little love for her mother and none for her father. She knew he was far too occupied to have much interest in her, and she knew he was a man incapable of affection. When he said that she should stay at the school for another year, she agreed.

At the end of the year, she arrived in Rome. Grandi was far too occupied to give her any attention. He gave her a generous allowance, made her a member of various high class clubs, checked to see that she had amusing and well born friends, then left her to her own devices. Every month, he arranged to take her to a stately, dull dinner at Alfredo's. When he had time to think of her, he imagined she was thoroughly enjoying herself, and was behaving as the daughter of the richest man in Italy should behave herself.

When he read of the kidnapping and about the club,

he flew into a towering rage. He had her locked in one of the upper guest rooms, and called for an inquiry to be made of her past activities. A discreet detective agency produced a report that Grandi could scarcely believe. She had not only been behaving like a whore, but was on drugs. There was also a serious possibility now of further kidnap attempts.

Grandi decided to remove Gina from the Italian scene. One of his aides found Orchid villa and Grandi rented it. The electrified fence was installed and all the security gimmicks, and within a month, Gina was taken there by her father and Frenzi Amando.

Gina was too awed by her father's fury to think of protesting. She had no idea who Amando was, but she hated the sight of him.

Before leaving her to return to Rome, Grandi talked to her.

'You have behaved disgracefully,' he said. 'You will remain here until I decide when you are fit to mix with decent people. If, at the end of a year, I get a good report about you, I will then consider giving you supervised freedom. You have betrayed my trust in you, and no one does that without bitterly regretting it.'

Gina moved uneasily. How she hated her father! To have done this to her! To have her caged behind an electrified fence, to have this cold blooded, snake of a man as her custodian! This man continually watched her. She could feel his eyes on her now. He was probably watching her from one of the upper windows of the villa.

Although, from time to time, she missed drugs, she really suffered from the lack of lovers. Sex tormented her day and night.

Apart from the servants who scarcely spoke to her, there was this tough ex-cop who had as much sex in him as the gun on his hip. The other guard was revoltingly fat and he had a hairy wart on his nose. She was sure he was a voyeur. He was always watching her from behind shrubs, giving her leering smiles, his little eyes stripping her.

The one saving grace of this gilded cage was Suka, the Japanese general factotum who ran the villa. Although he was inscrutable, she sensed that he was sorry for her. It was Suka, as he was serving her tea, who told her that the guard Joe had been caught by Amando sleeping and had been dismissed.

'There is a new guard, signorina,' Suka said, and went away.

A new guard? Gina stretched her long legs. She knew better than to ask details. Suka was very careful about his relations with her. Both of them were aware that Amando could be watching.

Could this new guard be interesting? she wondered. God! How she needed an interesting man!

Her mind wandered back to those marvellous, erotic nights in Rome when she had so often shared a vast bed with two young, rich stags who took her, turn and turn about.

She was releasing a soft moan as she re-lived those exciting moments when she heard a gentle cough that made her open her eyes and half start up.

Suka was standing at her side, holding a tray on which stood a glass of tomato juice: she was forbidden any kind of alcoholic drink. As he placed the glass on the table, he said softly, without looking at her, 'Signor Amando goes to 'Frisco. Not back until tomorrow. Very important dinner.' He left her.

Gina drew in a deep breath. The new guard would be on duty! For the first time in days, she smiled.

* * *

Although the fried chicken looked excellent, Frost found he had no appetite. He pushed the food around on his plate, aware that Marvin was eating hungrily.

Since returning to the Grandi villa, Frost's mind had been in turmoil. He was in the hole for four thousand dollars! He had no possible hope of paying this sharp shooting sonofabitch, and he felt in his bones that Silk would insist on payment. He remembered his words: *I don't take on a match with a piker!* There seemed to be no solution except to throw up his job and get out of Paradise City. What a sucker he had been!

'Something bothering you, Mike?' Marvin asked as he pushed aside his empty plate.

'I'm fine . . . just not hungry.' Frost stood up. 'I guess I ate too much for lunch.' He looked at his strap watch. 'You signing off?'

'Yeah. There's a good movie on the tube. Watch out for Old Creepy,' then nodding, he left the guardroom.

Frost stacked the plates on the tray, and put the tray on a chair by the door. Then lighting a cigarette, he slumped down in the armchair, facing the TV monitors. Would Marcia get him out of this hole? he wondered. He decided she wouldn't. He couldn't imagine her giving him four thousand dollars to settle a crazy bet. That he couldn't imagine! There was something about Silk that made Frost uneasy. Silk looked the kind of vicious bastard who would alert a tough debt collecting service, and if Frost failed to pay up, he would get cornered one night by an experienced gang who could break both his arms. He knew all about the collection-of-debts-service. The only solution was to throw up this sweet job and return to New York.

He heard the door open behind him and he looked around. Suka was collecting the tray.

'Signor Amando has left for 'Frisco,' Suka murmured. 'He returns tomorrow,' and he went out, shutting the door.

Frost shrugged. Now that he would be forced to leave Paradise City, Amando could get screwed for all he cared. The drag was that by leaving after only two nights of duty, he wouldn't get paid. His money was running dangerously low. By the time he had paid for his air ticket to New York, he would have very little left. What the hell was he going to do in New York anyway? He had already looked for a job there, and nothing had come up. For the first time since he had left the Army, Frost began to be worried.

He was still worrying, staring at the monitors, when he heard a sound behind him. His hands dropped on to his gun butt as he got to his feet and he swung around in one swift movement.

A girl stood in the doorway, smiling at him.

Gina had watched Amando drive away in the Rolls, then she had taken a shower, hesitated before her vast wardrobe, then selected an emerald green cocktail dress that fitted snugly, revealing her curves: a dress she hadn't worn since leaving Rome. The dress could be unzipped for immediate action, and when going to a party, immediate action was what she wanted.

Frost's eyes opened wide as he looked at her. He guessed she was Gina Grandi. He hadn't expected her to be so spectacularly exciting. As his experienced eyes ran over her compact body, he knew she was naked under the dress.

'Hi!' she said. 'You're the new guard.'

Frost felt lust stir in him.

'Mike Frost,' he said. 'I know who you are.'

Gina regarded him. What a beautiful hunk of man! she thought, and moved into the room, closing the door behind her.

'Do you like the job . . . Mike?'

He scarcely heard what she was saying. He knew for sure that she could be taken. His experience with women over the years had taught him to know the signs, and the green light was flashing.

'I like it a lot better now,' he said. He didn't hesitate. What had he to lose? He walked to her while she stood, waiting, and when he reached her, she slid her arms around his neck and thrust her body hard against his. His lips came down on hers and her tongue darted. They stood, straining against each other for a long moment, then she pushed him away, smiling at him.

'Let's have fun, Mike. Not here . . . in my room.'

Holding his wrist, she pulled him into the big lobby and up the broad stairs, along a corridor and into her spacious bedroom.

She was naked and lying across the bed as Frost shut the door.

* * *

Frost came awake as the clock downstairs chimed two. Hard, white moonlight came through the big window and lit up the bed. He looked down at the sleeping girl at his side. A beauty, he thought, what a beauty! He lay back on the pillow and stretched his long legs, then he thought of Silk. He felt vicious hatred run through him. If it hadn't been for that crazy bet, he would be home and dry, but now he would be leaving as soon as Marvin took over the guard duty. He would be leaving this sweet job, and worst still, leaving this little nympho who had given herself to him with abandoned savageness. His right shoulder was still bleeding slightly where she had bitten him. His loins ached. He felt as if he had been fed through a rock crusher.

He turned on his side and regarded the girl, lit by the moonlight. As he was admiring her, her eyes opened, and she stretched like a sleek, beautiful cat.

Then it was her turn to regard him. What a man! she thought, and her mind became busy to find the solution as to how they could have many more nights like this. That sonofabitch Amando! This was the first time he had left the villa – after nearly four months! When would he go again? She wanted and needed this hunk of male excitement, lying by her side, every night!

'Hi,' Frost said.

She slid her arms around him and rolled over on top of him. She began to nibble at his lips, but Frost was drained. Marcia had practically demolished him, and now Gina's fierce love making had reduced him to nothing. Firmly, he pushed her away.

'That's it, baby,' he said. 'I've got to get back to work. This is hello and goodbye. Tomorrow, I'm quitting.'

She stared at him, then sat up.

'Quitting? What do you mean?'

Frost swung his legs off the bed.

'I'm throwing up this job.' He stood up, flexing his muscles, then began to dress.

Gina stared at him in dismay, regarding his lean brown body and his muscles.

'Mike! What are you saying? Why are you leaving?'

He zipped up his trousers, then sat on the bed.

'I'm leaving because I've been taken for a sucker,' then he went on to tell her about the shooting match and about Silk. 'I now owe this jerk four thousand bucks,' he concluded. 'There's no way I can pay him. So . . . I have to get out of town before he puts on the squeeze.'

She caught hold of his hand.

'You must be kidding, Mike! Four thousand? That's nothing!'

'That's your thinking. To me, that kind of money is a lump. I'm getting out or else I'll land up with a broken arm.'

'A broken arm? What are you saying?'

He gave her a wry grin.

'Forget it, baby. This isn't your scene. I'm quitting tomorrow.' He stood up. 'So long, baby, and thanks.'

'Mike!' Her voice was shrill.

He paused at the door.

'Wait!'

She scrambled off the bed, ran to a big closet, jerked open the door and fumbled in a drawer, then she swung around and came to him, smiling.

'Here, take it! It's worth at least twenty thousand. My fink of a father gave it to me for my birthday,' and she dropped a diamond and emerald ring into his hand. 'Hock it, Mike. Pay off this jerk. I couldn't care less about the ring.

Frost stared at the ring, hesitated, then grinned. Why

not? Here was the solution to get Silk off his back and to keep this job. What did a ring like this mean to this corrupt, little nympho?

'You really mean you want to bail me out, baby?' he said, dropping the ring into his pocket.

'I want you to stay here,' she said breathlessly, and put her arms around his neck, thrusting her body against his. 'I want many more nights.'

'Okay.' Frost slid his hands down her naked back and pulled her closer. 'I'll fix it.' Then pushing her away, he left the room and ran silently down the stairs and into the guardroom.

He came to an abrupt standstill as he saw Suka sitting in the armchair, facing the monitors. Hearing him, Suka got to his feet, his face expressionless, and moved by Frost.

'What the hell are you doing here?' Frost demanded.

'Guarding,' Suka said, and went out of the room.

Frost stared after him, frowning, then shrugged. He dropped into the armchair, and taking out the ring Gina had given him, he examined it. Twenty thousand! Well, for God's sake!

When Marvin relieved him at 08.00, Frost went to his cabin and slept for four hours, then after a sandwich lunch, completely forgetting he had a date with Marcia at the Spanish Bay hotel at midday, he drove to Paradise City, unaware that a cream coloured Mercedes, driven by a swarthy, fat man wearing sun goggles, had moved after him.

Mitch Goble had been waiting in a parking bay within sight of the guard barrier leading to Paradise Largo since 09.00, waiting for Frost to appear. He had spent the three hour wait reading a 'girlie' magazine. He was a man of infinite patience, also a man with a gross appetite. He had with him a paper sack of cheeseburgers, and from time to time, he dipped into the sack.

Frost found a hock shop on Seaview boulevard.

He had his glib story ready.

54

'My wife and I are parting,' he said to the thin, Jewish clerk who was standing behind the counter. 'We need fast money.' He put the ring on the counter. 'I paid twenty thousand for this.'

The clerk examined the ring, sighed, said it was worth only fifteen thousand, and he would lend six for three months.

Frost was in no mood to haggle. After all, it wasn't his ring. He took the money and the ticket, and as he walked back to where he had parked the T.R., he remembered his date with Marcia. The time now was 13.25. He decided she had probably gone to the restaurant. He couldn't imagine she would wait around for any man, so he headed for the restaurant.

Mitch Goble walked into the hock shop.

'Hi, Issy,' he said. 'What gives with that guy who's just left?'

Issy, who was terrified of Goble, produced the ring.

'He's hocked it for six. It's worth at least thirty.'

Goble examined the ring, grunted, then handed it back.

'Keep your nose clean, Jew-boy,' he said, and leaving the shop, he shut himself in a telephone booth. He called Silk.

'Our creep has just hocked a thirty thousand diamond and emerald ring for six grand,' he told Silk. 'He's heading your way.'

'Take time off, Mitch,' Silk said, and he hung up.

After waiting until half past twelve, Marcia had telephoned Silk from her hotel.

'He hasn't shown,' she said. 'So what do I do?'

'Come over here,' Silk said. 'No problem.'

When Frost walked into the restaurant, he was met by Ross Umney who had been told by Silk to look out for him.

'Hi, Mike!' Umney said with his wide, friendly smile. 'Marcia's just arrived. She's asking for you.'

'I've got business,' Frost said curtly. 'Is Silk around?'

'Sure . . . down in the shooting gallery.'

Shoving past Umney, Frost took the elevator down to the basement. He found Silk talking to Moses. As soon as Moses saw Frost, he moved away and began busying himself cleaning guns.

Frost planted himself before Silk.

'I owe you four,' he said, and taking out his wallet, he extracted four one thousand dollar bills and thrust them at Silk.

'No, you don't friend,' Silk said, and his thin lips moved into what could be taken for a smile. 'We got our lines crossed. That stupid hunkhead, Ross, should have told me. How was I to know you are a friend of my niece?'

Frost stared at him.

'Your niece?'

'Yeah . . . Marcia. When she heard I'd taken you for a ride, she beat the ears off me.' He laughed. 'I apologise, Mike. I didn't know you're one of us. You owe me nothing.'

Frost felt a rush of blood to his head.

'We made a bet. I don't give a damn who you are. I pay my debts!'

Silk continued to smile.

'Take it easy, friend,' he said. 'I run a racket here. I shoot for a living. I con suckers, but not friends. I apologise. Okay?'

Frost hesitated, then relaxed.

'You sure can shoot. Okay.'

Silk nodded.

'We fast buck folk are all in some racket,' he said, and taking out a pack of cigarettes, he offered it. 'Marcia tells me you're guarding the Grandi babe.' He laughed. 'Some racket! Some babe!'

Frost grinned. He was so relieved that he hadn't to part with four thousand dollars, his previous assessment that Silk could be dangerous began to fade. Also he liked Silk's remark about 'fast buck folk'. That's what he was: hunting for the fast buck.

'That's a fact,' he said. 'Well, it's a job.' He put the

bills back into his wallet. A thought dropped into his mind. He would tell Gina he had paid his debt, give her two thousand and the hock ticket, and keep the four thousand for himself.

A heavily built man came out of the elevator and moved towards Silk.

'Hi, Lu,' he said. 'You want a little bet?'

Silk went into his senile act.

'You bet too high for me, Mr Lewishon.'

'Aw, come on! Four to one with target rifles.'

Frost headed for the elevator. Some racket! he thought. What the hell was he doing, sitting in a guardroom at six hundred a week! He was sure Silk would be picking up four thousand in the next half hour!

Ross Umney was hanging around the elevator as Frost reached the restaurant floor.

'You want to eat, Mike?' he asked.

'I've already eaten. Where's Marcia?'

'Tied up right now.' Umney leered. 'A girl has to work. I want you to meet a good friend of mine. He's got influence.'

Umney linked his arm into Frost's arm and led him down a corridor, opened a door and led him into a small room where Mitch Goble was waiting.

Goble was chewing his way through a vast hamburger. He wiped his fat fingers on a serviette, got to his feet, and beamed at Frost.

'Mitch, I want you to meet a good friend of Marcia's,' Umney said. 'Mike Frost.'

Goble extended his hand.

'A pleasure, Mike. I've heard about you . . . you're one of us people.'

They all sat down at the table.

'Have a drink?' Umney said and snapped his fingers.

A waiter appeared.

'Scotch?' Umney asked, looking at Frost who nodded. Frost was regarding Goble, unable to place him. His clothes were casual but expensive. His fat, swarthy face

57

wasn't prepossessing, and, Frost thought, the genial smile could be a front.

'How are you liking this little City?' Goble asked.

'Fine.'

'Yeah . . . you've got yourself a sweet location,' Goble went on. 'The Grandi's pad must be quite something. You like it?'

'Who wouldn't?' Frost had a feeling that Goble was probing. During his service with the N.Y. cops, he had often run into men like Goble: smooth, dangerous operators. He decided to do some probing himself. 'What's your racket?'

The waiter arrived with the drinks, then he whispered something to Umney who scowled.

'Always something in this joint. Have to leave you boys. There's a creep who is moaning.' He tossed off his drink, patted Frost on his shoulder, said, 'Mitch'll look after you,' and he left.

Frost remembered the same performance when Umney had left him alone with Silk. He became very alert.

'My racket?' Goble said, and cut himself another hunk off his hamburger. 'I set up operations. Some guy comes to me and says he has an idea to make dough, what do I think about it? I look at the operation and tell him yes or no. Call me the outside man looking in.'

'Is that right?' Frost sipped his drink. 'Get you anywhere?'

'Oh, sure. We fast buck folk squeeze up a living.' Goble laughed. 'Marcia tells me you're taking care of the Grandi babe. Only last week, I had a guy with a nutty idea he could snatch that babe and pick up twenty million dollars. I told him he should get his head examined.' He paused and stared directly at Frost. 'Right?'

Frost felt a prickle run up his spine.

'Right . . . what?'

Goble paused to finish the hamburger, sighed, then shook his head.

'No way to snatch the babe,' he said. 'Right?'

'Your guy can try,' Frost said quietly. 'He can get himself torn to pieces by four Doberman Pinschers. If the dogs don't get him, I will.'

Goble put a surprised look on his face.

'Dogs, huh? Still, dogs can be taken care of.' He looked reflective. 'Twenty million bucks! That's real bread!'

Twenty million! Frost thought. Yes, Grandi would pay that to get his daughter back.

'Anyway, Mike, I told this guy to forget it,' Goble went on. 'I once had the same idea, and I cased the joint . . . no way. This wop fink has really taken care of it.'

'You can say that again.'

'Yeah.' Goble sipped his drink. 'Since then I've thought about it. There's no problem that can't be solved. Twenty million! Bread like that gives me daydreams. Just suppose four smart operators really got together. Suppose they did snatch this babe. That'd be five million each.'

Five million! Frost thought. That kind of money would set him up for life! He kept his expression deadpan as he said, 'You just said there was no way.'

'I thought that a couple of months ago,' Goble said. 'I keep thinking. It doesn't hurt me to think.' He looked at Frost, then said, 'The Trojan horse.'

Frost frowned.

'What the hell does that mean?'

'My old man was a nut about Greek history,' Goble said. 'He bent my ears with all this gaff about the Greeks. There was a fink called Ulysses. The Greeks were besieging the Trojans and getting nowhere. This fink made a big wooden horse and he put soldiers in it and he kidded the Trojans they would be sitting pretty if the horse was put in the city. The jerks fell for it. The soldiers spilled out at night and opened the gates and the Trojans got skewered. To snatch this babe, I'd want a Trojan horse . . . an inside man: maybe one of the staff. They have ten people keeping that joint running. Maybe one of them could be got at.' He shrugged. 'I think. It's my job. Could be I also need my head examined.'

Frost stared at him. Was he being propositioned? Five million! He had come to Paradise City to make money, but to-date, he had only landed a job for six hundred a week . . . chick-feed! Goble had said, 'Maybe one of the staff could be got at.' That was a direct hint. Frost, looking at the fat man, was now sure he was being propositioned. This was something he needed to think about. Play hard to get, he told himself, as he got to his feet.

'Yeah . . . get your head examined,' he said curtly, and walked out, leaving his drink untouched.

Goble finished his drink, then reached for the drink Frost had left. Silk came silently into the room, closed the door and sat at the table. He had been listening to the conversation that had been relayed to him by a hidden microphone.

'Nice work, Mitch,' he said. 'You handled it just right.'

Goble nodded.

'So what now?'

'We'll give him time to think. He's a real fast worker. Hot pants gave him the ring – unless he stole it, but I don't dig that. Amando was away for the night. She wouldn't miss out on an opportunity like that. My guess is he screwed her, told her he was in the hole for four thousand, and to keep him, she gave him the ring.' Silk rubbed his bony hands together. 'It's moving our way, Mitch. We wait.'

Goble stared thoughtfully at Silk.

'Don't take this guy for a sucker, Lu. I've a feeling he could be tricky.'

Silk allowed a wintry smile to crease his face.

'I can be tricky too,' he said.

*   *   *

Five million dollars!

Frost had driven away from the restaurant and down to the beach. He had found himself an isolated spot under the shade of a palm tree, and had sat down on the sand to think.

The photo swam slowly into focus. The setup had begun with his chance meeting with Marcia – Silk's niece. Probably, she had been told to look out for a likely stooge. Probably, Silk had got inside information that the second guard wouldn't last long, so he had planned ahead. Maybe, Joe Solomon was working with Silk. He (Frost) must have seemed to Silk to be a gift from heaven.

The Trojan horse!

Silk had been smart enough to know there was no way of snatching Gina without an inside man, so he had picked on him.

Frost dug his fingers into the hot sand while he thought.

Five million dollars! Suppose he played along? Suppose Silk had a safe, working plan? Frost's eyes narrowed as he thought. Goble had talked of a fourth man – Umney? A four way split – five million dollars each. What he couldn't do with bread like that! Frost's thinking switched to Marvin. Suppose Gina was snatched? Would Grandi scream for the cops? Thinking about this, Frost decided he wouldn't. He would pay up, but Marvin, shrewd ex-cop as he was, would know there had to be an inside man, and he would point a finger at Frost.

It was one thing to snatch the girl, but something else beside, to get the ransom. When the ransom was paid and Gina returned, the heat would be on. Frost grimaced. He would be suspect number one. Silk must know this.

Frost let sand trickle through his fingers.

He wouldn't be Silk's stooge. If he was caught, he certainly wouldn't let Silk go free to spend the ransom. He would talk his head off, and Silk must know this.

Frost rubbed his hand over his sweating face. If he decided to act as the inside man, the snatch wouldn't be too difficult, but collecting and spending the ransom seemed to him, to be impossible.

He thought some more, but couldn't find a solution.

He felt sure that Silk wouldn't stick his neck out unless he had a foolproof plan. What was it?

For the next half hour, Frost sat staring at the glittering sea, his mind busy. Then, with a sudden nod of his head, he made his decision. He would pretend to play along with Silk, listen to Silk's plan, examine it, then opt out or opt in, depending how convincing Silk was.

As he got to his feet, he looked at his watch. The time was 15.15. He had five hours to kill before returning to the Grandi residence. He wondered if he should return to the Ace of Spades and see Marcia. He shook his head: play hard to get. He decided to take a closer look at Paradise City, and walked to where he had parked his car.

Five million dollars!

He kept thinking of owning such a sum. His mind was so occupied with visions of how he would spend money like that, he failed to observe a lean, tall youth with long greasy hair, a face like a ferret's, wearing a T shirt and dirty jeans, swing his leg over a powerful Honda motor-cycle and come after him as Frost drove on to the high-way and headed for the City.

This youth, known as Hi-Fi, worked for Mitch Goble. He was a heroin addict. Goble kept him supplied with just enough money to buy his next fix. Goble had told him to keep tracks on Frost and never let him out of his sight.

Still thinking about a possible future, Frost drove into Paradise City and parked the T.R. outside an amusement arcade. Leaving the car, he wandered into the arcade which was humming with activity. Crowds of young people jostled around spending their dimes, eating hot dogs, screaming at each other.

Frost jostled his way to the shooting range. A fat, smil-ing Polak handed him a rifle. It was a way to kill time, Frost thought as he settled himself and took aim at the distant target.

Hi-Fi melted into the crowd, his eyes on Frost's broad back.

Frost had taken the centre of the target out when he heard a voice say, 'You Frost?'

He lowered the rifle and turned to find a tall, wiry man, with a lined sun-tanned face and clear ice blue eyes at his side.

He knew at once that this man was a cop.

'That's me,' he said. 'Who are you?'

'Tom Lepski. City police,' Lepski grinned and offered his hand.

Lepski? Frost's mind became very alert. He remembered Marvin had said Lepski was a first grade detective, and a good friend of his. It had been Lepski who had told Marvin that Grandi had needed a bodyguard.

'Sure,' he said. 'Jack mentioned you.'

'Yeah. He and I are buddies,' Lepski said. 'I saw the T.R. out front, so I thought I'd meet you.'

'Glad you did.' Frost laid down the rifle. 'Just amusing myself.'

'Jack said you were some shot.' Lepski eyed the distant target. 'Yeah . . . you sure are. You got a minute? Suppose we go over to Joe's across the way for a beer?'

'Why not?'

As they left the arcade, Hi-Fi went after them. He watched them enter the bar across the street, hesitated, then walked fast to a telephone booth. He called Silk.

'Our creep is chatting it up with Lepski,' Hi-Fi reported.

Silk's face tightened. This was unexpected and bad news. Was Frost alerting the cops that Goble had propositioned him? After a moment's thought, he decided not. Five million, to a man like Frost, was too big a temptation for him to shoot off his mouth to a cop.

'Stay with him, but watch it,' Silk said, and hung up.

Settled at a corner table with beers before them, Lepski said, 'You've got yourself a sweet job.' He grinned. 'The City police are right behind Mr Grandi. He takes care of us, so we take care of him. His daughter stays safe.'

His face expressionless, Frost nodded.

'So Jack tells me.'

'Have you met her yet?'

Frost shook his head.

'Not yet. I'm on night duty this week. All I have to worry about is Amando.'

'There's a jerk.' Lepski grimaced. 'Nothing satisfies him. He bothers the Chief nearly every week. He has a bee in his nut that the girl is going to get snatched.' Lepski laughed. 'How can she? We keep explaining it to him, but he won't lie down.'

'It's his way of earning his money,' Frost said.

'I guess that's right.' Lepski's cop eyes swept over Frost. 'When we heard that Amando had given Joe Davis the gate, and he had reason, we got interested in you.' There was no smile now on Lepski's face. 'We heard you got the job through Joe Solomon. We know all about Joe. He's not our favourite citizen. So we leaned on Joe and he came up with your credentials. What we learned from them, satisfied us you were right for the job. We checked the N.Y.P.D. and the F.B.I. They gave you a clearance.' He paused, then went on, 'There's this thing that bothers us: you don't stay long with a job.' Again a pause, then he said, 'Maybe you've got itchy feet.'

Frost's mind worked swiftly. So the cops had put him under a microscope. He was too much of a cop himself to be leaned on.

'Are you asking a question or are you just talking?' he said quietly.

'Call it a question.'

Frost smiled.

'Tell me something, friend, are you asking this question because your Chief told you to ask it or are you just playing cop?'

Lepski stiffened. His Chief had given him no instructions to quiz Frost. He realised he had moved on to tricky ground.

He waved his hand airily.

'Don't get me wrong. Let me explain. We don't want

Gina Grandi snatched. Right now, we know she has total protection. There is no way to get at her unless there is an inside man, and if an inside man appears, she could get snatched. We have screened everyone living at the villa: all of them are okay. So you appear on the scene. So we screen you. Get the photo?'

Frost nodded.

'Sure . . . sure, but that doesn't answer my question.' He finished his beer. 'Are you interrogating me because you have instructions from your Chief or are you a first grade detective after further promotion?' He leaned forward, staring at Lepski. 'I've been on the force. I know how it works. I know all about guys who lean on people to get promotion. I did it myself, but nobody leans on me. So you talk to your Chief. Tell him, I'll tell him anything he wants to know. I have nothing to hide, but I don't – repeat don't – get leaned on by a first grade detective.' He got to his feet. 'Okay with you, Lepski?'

Lepski stared up at him, then before he could think of anything to say, Frost gave him a broad smile and walked out of the bar.

Hi-Fi was sitting astride his Honda as Frost walked to his car. He gunned the motor and moved into the traffic as Frost drove down the main street.

Frost's mind was busy. He was uneasy. Had he handled Lepski right? he asked himself. The last thing he wanted was to make an enemy of a cop, but he couldn't let Lepski lean on him. He shrugged. Maybe it wasn't important, but what was important was that the cops had reached the same conclusion as Silk had done: to snatch Gina, there had to be an inside man.

Frost drove aimlessly towards Miami. He still had some hours before returning to Villa Orchid. The traffic was light. He kept looking into his rear mirror as good drivers do, and he picked up Hi-Fi tooling along behind him. Hadn't he seen this creep before? Frost frowned. He remembered seeing him on the deserted beach when Frost had been sitting in the shade, thinking. Now here he was again. Was he being tailed? He grinned. He studied Hi-Fi in the driving mirror: a punk: one of Silk's stooges?

Reaching Miami, he swung off Bay-shore avenue and on to S.W. 17th avenue, then turned left on to Miami avenue. The Honda followed him.

So he was being tailed!

Frost doubled back and headed for Paradise City. He was relaxed, humming to himself.

On the outskirts of the City, he left the highway and drove down a sandy road to the beach. Leaving the car, he walked fast to a clump of sea palms, hearing the noise of the Honda as it came down the road.

He dropped out of sight on hands and knees and waited. He heard the Honda motor die.

Hi-Fi was nervous. Leaving his motorcycle, he walked slowly down the sandy path, sweat on his face. He had been told not to let Frost out of his sight. He knew if he didn't obey orders his heroin money would stop.

He reached a clearing and looked up and down the wide stretch of deserted beach, then Frost dropped on him, his knees smashing into Hi-Fi's back, slamming him on to the sand.

Hi-Fi let out a yell as hard, vicious fingers encircled his throat. He tried to struggle, but the fingers tightened.

'Take it easy, sonny,' Frost said quietly. 'Just answer questions. Are you from Silk?'

Hi-Fi wriggled, heaved and tried vainly to throw off the crushing weight that kept him flat on the sand.

'Don't act stupid, sonny.' Frost said and releasing his grip on Hi-Fi's throat, he grabbed his right wrist and put a lock on it. 'Talk or I'll bust your arm.'

Hi-Fi felt the pressure. The pain that shot up his arm nearly made him faint.

'Are you from Silk?' Frost asked him.

'Yeah . . . yeah. You're breaking my arm!' Hi-Fi moaned.

Frost released him and stood up. Hi-Fi lay still, then turned on his back, glaring up at Frost.

66

'Don't try a thing, sonny,' Frost said. 'Just go back to Silk and tell him I don't like being tailed. The next time I spot you following me, I'll break your arm. Okay?'

They looked at each other. Hi-Fi had often been in the hands of the police. He knew a cop when he saw one.

'Okay,' he mumbled, and watched Frost walk back across the sand to where he had left his car.

Four

Mitch Goble, a half eaten hotdog in his fat hand, stormed
into the room, overlooking the Ace of Spades' swimming
pool, where Silk and Umney had just finished a tray
dinner.

'Hi-Fi blew it!' Goble said, and sat down heavily at the
table, facing Silk. 'Frost caught him, gave him the treatment, and the little jerk shot with his mouth.'

Umney gave Silk a startled look, but Silk shrugged.

'So what? Frost is an ex-cop. He's smart. I wouldn't
have picked him unless I was sure he was smart. So, okay.
He now knows we are keeping tabs on him. Relax, Mitch.
It doesn't matter. We'll leave him alone. We wait.'

Goble finished his hotdog, wiped his mouth with the
back of his hand and eyed the debris on the two trays.

'I'm telling you, Lu, Frost could be too smart. He
bothers me.'

'We can't do without him.' Silk lit a cigarette. 'I can
handle him. Relax. We're doing all right. You planted
the seed. A guy like Frost is going to think what five million will mean to him. We give him time. In a couple of
days, he'll come here to screw Marcia . . . that will be his
reason for coming here, but he'll be looking to talk business. I'll be here to talk business. Once I convince him
he'll lay his mits on five million, he'll play.'

'Just watch him,' Mitch said. 'You're smart, I'm smart,
Ross is smart . . . just watch he isn't smarter.'

While they were talking, Frost was eating corn beef
hash with Jack Marvin.

'Ran into your buddy, Tom Lepski,' Frost was saying casually.

'That's right?' Marvin grinned. 'Now there's a shrewd, dedicated cop. When Chief Terrell retires, it's my bet Tom will be Chief of Police here. What a worker! He has ambition like a tiger with a hornet up his ass.'

'Yeah. He tried to give me the treatment,' Frost said quietly. 'I cut him down to size.'

Marvin paused in his eating and regarded Frost.

'What does that mean?'

'Your buddy started throwing questions. The boys have been making inquiries about me – fair enough. He said they were bothered that I didn't stay with any job long. I've nothing to hide, but I don't get leaned on by an ambitious cop. So I leaned on him. If the Chief wants answers, he has only to ask. I don't dig answering questions from a first grade detective.'

Marvin rubbed his jaw as he laid down his knife.

'Maybe you played it wrong, Mike. Tom's a little touchy: better to have him as a friend than an enemy.'

'I've nothing to be nervous about,' Frost said curtly and pushed back his chair. 'Between you and me, I don't give a damn about your buddy. I read him. He's ambitious . . . so was I when I was on the force. Okay, but no one leans on me.' He stood up, stretched, then went on, 'Nothing happen today?'

Looking a little worried, Marvin got to his feet.

'The same old routine. She must be goddamn lonely. I'm sorry for her. She spent the afternoon with the dogs. She can handle them better than I can.'

Frost registered this piece of news.

'Those tigers dig her?'

'They love her the way kids love candy. She's got a way with animals.'

And a way with men, Frost thought.

When Marvin had left and Suka had collected the trays, silently, not looking at Frost, except to bow slightly in his direction, Frost went over to the signal panel by the monitors and studied it.

Up to now, he hadn't bothered to look at the panel carefully. The top row of red lights indicated any break-in attempt. The next row were switches marked: *Fence neutraliser. Cabin 1 & 2 alarms. Dog whistle. F.A. alarm.* Below these switches were red lights marked: *Police alarm, F.B.I. alarm. Fire alarm.* Below these lights, were green lights and switches marked *Neutralisers for all alarms.*

Frost guessed the *F.A. alarm* was the alarm switch direct to Amando's sleeping quarters.

The Trojan horse!

With a flick of a few switches, the Grandi estate would become vulnerable!

He settled in the chair before the monitors, lit a cigarette and thought about Silk: a dangerous, deadly man. Frost moved uneasily. Suppose he agreed to be the inside man? Once Silk got his hands on Gina, what was to stop him putting a slug into Frost? Again Frost moved uneasily. He now knew Silk was a better shot than he was. If he acted as the inside man, how could he be sure of getting the five million and getting away with his life? How could Silk also be sure of getting away with the ransom?

Frost stubbed out his cigarette, frowning. He needed to know what Silk's plan was, then, if he decided to be the inside man, how he could safeguard himself and his share of the money? He was still brooding on the problem when he heard a sharp knock on the door behind him, then the door swung open.

Amando came in.

'All quiet, Frost?' he asked, in his low hissing voice.

Frost got to his feet. At least this snake of a man hadn't crept up on him, he thought, and hid a grin. He had thrown a scare into him.

'Yes, sir,' he said. 'Nothing to report.'

Amando nodded, his suspicious black eyes running over Frost.

'Keep alert. Mr Grandi will be coming at the end of the week. He will want to see you.'

'Yes, sir.'

Again Amando eyed him.

'This isn't much of a job for a man of your physique. I've been studying your record. You don't seem to keep jobs for long.'

'I like changes, sir,' Frost said quietly. 'Security work offers changes, that's why I went in for it. I guess this job isn't permanent, is it?'

'No, I wouldn't say it's permanent. I trust Miss Grandi will be out of danger in a few months' time.'

'I'm glad you think so, sir. From my experience Miss Grandi must always be in some degree of danger.'

Amando stared thoughtfully at him, nodded, and went away.

When Marvin came in at 08.00, Frost told him what Amando had said.

'Looks like you're going to lose your job you like so much, Jack,' he said.

Marvin grimaced.

'You were right to tell him. As long as there are billions lying around, so there will be an attempted snatch.' He put the coffee percolator on. 'But maybe Grandi is realising he can't keep her penned up like this, but what the solution is beats me.'

'That's Grandi's headache,' Frost said. 'Me for bed.'

After a four hour sleep, he shaved, showered, then called the Spanish Bay hotel. He asked to speak to Miss Goolden.

Marcia came on the line so quickly, Frost grinned to himself.

'Why, honey, where have you been?' she asked. 'I've missed you.'

'That makes two of us. Look, baby, how about spending the afternoon on the beach? I'm not in the mood for plush luxury. Bring a swim suit, and let's get lost some place.'

'Sure, darling. Marvellous! Suppose you pick me up at two o'clock.'

'But maybe you're too busy,' Frost said, grinning. 'Just say the word. I'll understand.'

Her instructions from Silk had been clear: *stay with him; keep him hooked.*

'No problem, darling. I'll be waiting. 'Bye now,' and she hung up. She immediately called Silk. 'He wants to go swimming with me. He says he's not in the mood for plush luxury.'

'He's just playing hard to get,' Silk said. 'Now, here's how you handle him.'

Marcia listened, her expression tense, then when Silk had finished talking, she said, 'Okay, I'll do it, but he bothers me. There's something about him I don't trust.'

Silk laughed. It was a mirthless sound that always sent a chill up Marcia's spine.

'Since when have you ever trusted any man?' he said, then after a pause, he went on. 'This is important, chick. Don't foul it.' The threat in his voice was unmistakable. He hung up.

Marcia closed her eyes, feeling a shiver run through her as she replaced the receiver. Silk had instilled such terror into her as to leave her defenceless. Some years back, Ross Umney had come to see her when she had the apartment in Miami. Although he didn't say so, she knew he had come on Silk's instructions.

'I want to spell this out to you,' Umney said, after settling in an armchair. 'Lu is a professional killer. He makes his living knocking off creeps who get in the way. He's not a guy to fool with. He thinks you can be useful to him, as I am useful, and as Mitch is useful. So when he needs a silk pussy to setup a creep, you're going to be it.'

After four years as a call girl, Marcia had developed into a very confident, tough cookie. She laughed.

'Tell Uncle Lu to go screw himself. I'm not working for anyone but myself. Up on the feet, handsome, and blow.'

Umney smiled sadly.

'Come on, honey, you should know better than that. He needs a silk pussy. Before you, he tried a couple of chicks, but they said just what you just said.' He took from his wallet two coloured prints and leaning forward, dropped them into her lap. 'That's what he did to them. Lu's an acid expert.'

The prints were so horrifying, Marcia dropped them as if they were red hot.

Shuddering, she stared at Umney.

'He wouldn't do that to me . . . I'm his niece.'

'He'd do it to his own mother if she didn't co-operate,' Umney said with his sad smile. 'When he needs you, you jump. That's the way it is, honey, unless you want to lose your looks,' and he had left her.

Marcia had picked up the prints and studied them, shuddered, then tore them to bits. From that moment, she was Silk's slave. Her greatest pleasure had always been to stand before a mirror, admiring her beauty. To be reduced to a freak like those two girls was something she just couldn't take.

A year later, she had a telephone call from Silk.

'Go to apartment fourteen at the Sheraton at nine to-night chick,' he said. 'You are expected. Give the creep value for his money. Ross will give you a pill. Drop it in-to the creep's drink. When he's asleep, get out. Easy, isn't it?' A pause, then the threat in his voice. 'Don't foul it up.'

Umney had arrived and had given her a tiny envelope containing a yellow tablet.

'Careful, honey, of your looks,' he said.

She read in the next morning's *Paradise Herald* that a Mr Ballinski had been found dead in bed. Apparently, he had shot himself. He had been under considerable financial pressure. Mr Herman Radnitz, the well-known financier, had put in a bid to take over Mr Ballinski's company. Mr Ballinski had declared that only over his dead body would Mr Radnitz succeed. The company was failing through lack of management control. The financial editor of the *Paradise Herald* thought Mr Radnitz could revitalise the company, and in despair, knowing this, Mr Ballinski had shot himself.

Shuddering, Marcia now realised she was an accessory to murder.

Another year later, she had been instructed by Silk to set up another financier. She obeyed his instructions, but didn't look at the morning paper. She couldn't bear to know that this financier was also dead.

Then she had inherited the Ace of Spades restaurant. Free at last! she had foolishly thought, but Silk had come to her. He told her the Ace of Spades would make a suitable headquarters for him. Caught in the web of terror, Marcia had given over four of the rooms above the restaurant to him, Umney and Goble. The three of them had moved in, and she was stuck with them.

There had been no activity for her from Silk for the past four months, and she began to hope Silk no longer needed her, but would let her run the restaurant and her call girl service and leave her alone. Now, this crazy, dangerous kidnap idea, and she was right in the middle of it!

Silk had said in his quiet deadly voice, 'We need this guy, chick. You hook him, and keep him hooked. Understand?'

Yes, she understood. Those horrifying photographs were still very much alive in her mind.

Now, after a swim, she lay in her wet bikini beside Frost under the shade of palm trees. In the far distance, people disported themselves in the sea and on the beach, but where she and Frost were lying, they were isolated.

Frost seemed remote. He was smoking a cigarette, his eyes closed. She looked at him, worrying, then deciding she must take action, she moved her hand gently on his crotch. His reaction was instant. He swept away her hand and sat up.

'Let's talk,' he said, looking down at her. 'You're not here for fun and games? Right?'

She tried to make her eyes register surprise.

'What are you saying, honey?'

'I said let's talk,' Frost said. 'Silk needs me. I've figured it. You're his niece, so you work with him. You are a whore. The sex stuff means nothing to you. Fair enough, but don't get the idea you're conning me. That's what I am saying.'

Marcia again thought of those horrifying prints. She sat up, crossing her arms around her knees.

'Yes, Silk needs you, and I need you, Mike,' she said quietly. 'My restaurant is in the red. I thought it was going to be my life-line. Without an injection of money, it's going to fold. Lu came up with this idea of getting a big ransom from Grandi. The way he has it figured, it will work, but not without you. Your take will be five million. If you want money like that, then talk to Lu. It's as simple as that.'

'How has he got it figured?' Frost asked, regarding her.

'He'll tell you.'

'Has he told you?'

She shook her head.

'I wouldn't want to know, Mike. My job was to find you. I talked to a lot of guys before deciding you were the one Lu needed. For finding you I get five hundred thousand. With that kind of money, my restaurant will survive.'

'What makes you think that Silk will give you the money if he does get the ransom?'

'You don't have to worry about your share, Mike. Silk is a professional. He's no piker. He'll pay me, and he'll pay you. That's the least you have to worry about.'

'What else would I have to worry about?' Frost asked, stubbing out his cigarette.

'He'll tell you.'

Frost lit another cigarette while he stared at the distant sea. Five million dollars! What had he to lose to talk to Silk? If Silk couldn't convince him, then he would opt out.

'Okay, so I'll listen, but that doesn't mean I'll be his inside man,' he said.

Marcia drew in a deep breath of relief.

'No time like the present,' she said. 'Let's go. He's at the restaurant now.'

'Let him sweat,' Frost said, then pointing at her bikini, he went on, 'Why are you wearing that?'

Men! Marcia thought as she unstrapped the clips. God! What animals they are!

* * *

They sat around the big table in the room above the swimming pool. Silk was flanked either side by Umney and Goble. Frost sat at the far end of the table on which stood drinks, two bottles of Scotch and a tray of canapes. Goble was the only one to eat. Every so often his fingers closed on one of the elaborate tid-bits which he conveyed to his mouth.

'I've been working on this idea for some time,' Silk was saying, staring at Frost. 'There's a twenty million rake off, but there's no way to get at the girl without an inside man. I'm offering you the job for a five million cut.'

Frost turned his tumbler of Scotch around in his fingers.

'I was talking to 1st Grade Detective Lepski,' he said. 'I'm told he is a very smart cop. Let me quote what he said. These were his words: "We don't want Gina Grandi snatched. Grandi looks after us, so we look after him. Right now, we know she has total protection. There is no way to get at her unless there is an inside man, and if an inside man appears, she could get snatched." ' Frost paused and stared at Silk. 'Those were his words. So I opt to be the inside man, she gets snatched, and the heat drops on me. That's not my idea of picking up five million.'

Silk smiled.

'It wouldn't be mine either, but the heat won't drop on you, Mike. It'll drop on Jack Marvin.'

Frost stiffened.

'Marvin? That's crazy talk! Now listen to me . . .'

Silk raised his hand.

'Relax. I've thought this thing out. I've lived in this

City for fifteen years, and I know all about the cops here. They know their business. I guess they are about the best. From the start of my thinking, I knew that when the girl's snatched, they would know there had to be an inside man. I knew they would look hard at the man who replaced Joe Davis. Now listen carefully, Mike, I protect my organisation. You ask Ross and Mitch. I've never let them down.' He looked to right and left. 'Right?'

'You can say that again,' Goble said, stuffing a sardine on toast into his mouth.

Umney nodded.

'So okay,' Silk went on. 'The cops have two likely suspects for the inside man: you and Marvin. I'm going to fix it they turn the heat on Marvin.'

Frost was leaning forward, his eyes intent.

'Keep talking. How do you turn the heat on Marvin? Let me tell you something first. Lepski and Marvin are buddies. Marvin has a gold-plated reputation for being a dedicated, straight ex-cop. Your thinking's cock-eyed.'

Again Silk smiled.

'When the take is twenty million, who is ever straight and dedicated?'

'Five million,' Frost said.

'No, twenty million. Marvin will seem to handle the snatch on his own. Here's how the cops will see it. One night, Marvin decides to snatch the girl. The twenty million take has been too much of a temptation. It's all in his favour. He will have no trouble handling the dogs. No problem there. He will be on night duty. You will be sleeping in your cabin. You don't present a problem. He goes to the girl's room, knocks her on the head, carries her down to the harbour, puts her in the motorboat and away he goes. The following morning you go to relieve him: no Marvin. You raise the alarm: no Gina. Amando will alert Grandi. You stand by for orders. Grandi reads the kidnap note: pay up, no cops or your daughter gets knocked off. Grandi won't call in the cops. He waits. Then Marvin telephones. He gives instructions how the ransom is to be

77

paid and he says you are the one he will deal with. Grandi delivers, and you give me the ransom, then you return, still the white headed boy.' He paused. 'How do you like it so far?'

'It stinks,' Frost said, but his heart was thumping. 'You say Marvin telephones. Amando will take the call. Marvin's voice is very special. You can't mistake it, and don't tell me Marvin would co-operate. You would have to fake it, and that's out.'

Again Silk smiled.

'Marvin will co-operate. When I make a plan, it's organised. For three months, Ross has been studying Marvin. Here's something you don't know. Marvin's marriage didn't work, but he has a son, aged three. We can get that kid. No problem there. Marvin will co-operate.'

Frost shifted in his chair, his mind very alert.

'So, okay, the heat's off me, and on Marvin,' he said. 'Grandi gives me the ransom, and I deliver it to you. This is fine, so far, for you, but how about me? You three could take off, and I'm the sucker.'

Silk poured a little more Scotch into his glass and added charge water.

'You're not using your head,' he said. 'Never mind! I'll show you your share will be guaranteed. I'll deal with that later. Now I'll tell you what really happens: not what the cops think has happened, but what does happen.'

'I'm listening,' Frost said.

'There are some details that have to be ironed out, but here is the general idea. You take night duty for a week, then change with Marvin? Right?'

Frost nodded.

'Okay, so you are on day duty, and Marvin on night duty when we snatch the girl. What time do you finish your day duty?'

'Twenty hours. Then we have dinner together, and I am free.'

'What's the girl doing? Does she eat alone?'

'Maybe. I don't know. She could eat with Amando, but I doubt it.'

'That's something I want you to find out. I'll give you knock out pills. They are special: delayed action. Your job is to put a pill in Marvin's drink, Amando's drink and the girl's drink. How you do this is up to you.' Silk gave a wry grin. 'You must expect to earn five million dollars, but let's leave that for the moment. If you can't dope their drinks, the operation won't work, but knowing you are smart, I am sure you will fix it. Okay, the pills take six hours to work, and when they work, it's a complete knock-out. So the girl, Amando and Marvin are knocked out. Suppose you fix the drinks at eight o'clock, then at two o'clock, you go to the guardroom where Marvin is snoring his head off, and you neutralise the fence and get the dogs back into their compound. It just means pressing the right buttons... right?'

Frost gaped at him.

'How the hell do you know that?'

Silk waved his hand to Umney who was grinning.

'Ross gathers information. He chatted up the guy who fixed the electronics. Ross can get information out of a deaf mute. We know more about the electronic setup than you do. You get the dogs back in their compound and the fence neutralised. Then we three arrive by boat. No problem there. The snatch will take place at three-thirty in the morning. There'll be no one around. We take the girl and Marvin, both knocked out, to Grandi's motorboat, and away we go. Ross takes care of our boat.' Silk paused, then leaning forward, he went on, 'I'll spell it out. Your job is to dope the drinks, neutralise the dogs and the fence, and when you have done that you go back to bed. Not such a sweat for five million, is it?'

Frost thought about this, then he said, 'Very smart, but it still stinks to me. As I see it, you could get the girl, but what happens when the ransom is paid?' He pointed a finger at Silk. 'Once the ransom is paid and Grandi gets the girl back, he's going to call the cops. Once the cops

take over, the fun begins. As soon as you release Marvin,
he'll talk. He has an unshakeable reputation. When he
says he was doped, the cops will believe him, so the heat
comes back to me. Thought of that?'

Silk sipped his Scotch.

'Did I say anything about Marvin being released?'

Frost stared at the cold, ruthless face, and he felt a cold
shiver run up his spine.

'This is a twenty million dollar take,' Silk went on
softly. 'You don't have to worry about Marvin.' His
scarred face was like a stone mask. 'I'll take care of him.
Marvin will never be found, and the heat will always
remain on him. Get the photo?'

Frost felt his heart lurch a beat. So this was not only
going to be a twenty million dollar snatch, it was also
going to be a murder rap. He had done a lot of shady things
in the past, but he had stopped short of murder. Then his
mind switched to the prospects of owning five million
dollars. Marvin meant nothing to him. Five million!

'So, okay,' he said, 'I don't have to worry about Marvin.'
He found his mouth was so dry, he took a drink. 'And
Gina?'

'No problem there,' Silk said, easing himself back in his
chair. 'She gets returned. She's been doped. She will know
nothing. She'll be under sedation until she arrives back
home. No problem.'

'Where are you going to keep her until the ransom is
paid?'

'That's taken care of,' Silk said. 'Again no problem.'

'But where? I want to know,' Frost persisted.

Silk stared at him. His one eye suddenly went dull, but
his glass eye caught the sun coming through the big
window, and the glass eye glittered.

'First things first,' he said. 'How are you reacting? From
what I've spelled out, do you think we can snatch the
girl?'

Frost turned the glass of Scotch around and around in
his sweating fingers while he thought. Goble began to

chew on a lobster tail. Umney, leaning back in his chair, stretched his muscular arms and yawned. Silk, motionless, continued to stare at Frost.

After a long pause, Frost said, 'Given the breaks, yes. But there are complications. The dogs are a problem. I have a hundred yards walk from my cabin to the guard-room to fix the neutralisers. The dogs could nail me before I reached the guardroom. I also have a problem doping the drinks.'

Silk's lips moved into a smiling grimace.

'Those, of course, are the reasons why you earn five million dollars. I picked on you, because you're smart.' He sipped his drink, then putting down the glass, he went on, 'I now ask you, are you in or out?'

Again Frost thought of Marvin. Murder! Then he again thought of owning five million dollars.

He finished his drink, then set down the empty glass.

'We haven't talked about the ransom yet,' he said. 'To me, that's the sixty-four thousand dollar question. Convince me I can get five million and spend it in safety, and then I'll tell you if I'm in or out.'

Silk studied him for a long moment, then he waved his hands towards Umney and Goble.

'Okay, boys, grab some fresh air,' he said.

Umney got to his feet and moved to the door. Goble grabbed two canapes and followed Umney from the room.

Silk sipped his drink, lit a cigarette, then looked directly at Frost.

'So we're on our own,' he said. 'This is strictly between you and me. I am doing this job, with or without your help. You ask about the ransom. As you say, this is the sixty-four thousand dollar question. Before I even began to make plans to snatch this girl, I solved that question. What is the use of getting twenty million dollars if you can't spend it? I've now got it so fixed we can spend it, and that includes you. If I tell you how I have fixed it, you will have reached the point of no return, as Ross and Mitch have already reached the point of no return. If they lose

81

their nerve and back out, they know I will kill them,' Silk smiled. 'I earn my living killing people. Ross and Mitch know that, so you had better know it too. Before I tell you how I have fixed the ransom, I want you to think about what I have told you so far. Now, it is your turn to convince me I've picked the right inside man. I will want to know how you will handle the dogs: how you will dope Marvin, Amando and the girl, and how you will neutralise the fence. When you have convinced me you can do all this, and when you have told me you will work with me, then I'll tell you how I've fixed the ransom, and I assure you, I have fixed it.'

Frost hesitated, then shrugged.

'Well, okay, so I exercise my brain,' and he pushed back his chair.

'You do that,' Silk said. 'Let's get the record straight. If you haven't the brains nor the guts to work with me, you are no good to me, nor to yourself. I am guaranteeing you five million, and I don't give five million away to a pea-brain. So, Saturday morning you come here and convince me you can handle the dogs, neutralise the fence and dope the drinks. You'll have to convince me, and I need convincing. So, okay, you convince me. Then you tell me if you opt in or out. If you opt in, you will have passed the point of no return. Then I will tell you how I've fixed the ransom, and I guarantee I have fixed it. But if you haven't the nerve and you opt out, you will leave Paradise City and you will keep your trap shut.' He tapped the table with his finger. 'Make no mistake about this: I'm going ahead with this job. I will have to find another guard. It'll mean waiting, but I've waited already. But suppose you think you can pick up some money by going to the cops and talking? Okay, so you go to the cops, and you tell them I'm getting set to snatch the girl.' Silk stubbed out his cigarette. 'If you do that, there will be no snatch, but I'll be in the clear. You have no proof that I am planning the snatch. It'll be your word against mine. The cops have nothing on me. So I tell them you are crazy in the head, but knowing the cops here, they'll put a tab on me, so, no snatch, and I'll lose five million bucks.' He leaned forward, his one eye glaring at Frost. 'If you talk to the cops, you won't live long. There's no hole anywhere deep enough for you to hide in. Be sure, I'll come after you. Be very sure of that, and I'll kill you.'

* * *

Frost spent the remaining two hours before he took over from Marvin, in his cabin, smoking and thinking.

Although he thought of what life would mean to him when he had five million dollars to spend, his main thinking was about Silk. During the short time he had been a detective, he had run into a number of dangerous thugs. He had also run into a few Mafia hit-men, but none of them compared with Silk. Frost knew Silk was a professional in the top echelon bracket, and he was deadly dangerous. *I will guarantee I have fixed the ransom.* This, coming from a man of Silk's calibre, meant, somehow, he had solved the ransom problem, and that meant that if Frost opted in, he would have five million dollars to spend. He was almost sure that if he opted out, he would never leave Paradise City alive. Silk would never take the risk that he (Frost) might talk. Frost moved uneasily. He would meet with an accident. He was sure of that. So . . . he nodded to himself, he would opt in.

Now, he had problems to solve: how to dope Marvin, Amando and Gina. This was the priority problem. The second problem was how to neutralise the dogs. This also presented difficulties. The neutralising of the fence was easy once Marvin was doped and the dogs out of the way.

Frost realised he would have to collect a lot of information before he could begin to solve these problems. He looked at his strap watch. The time was 19.45: time to go to the guardroom and have dinner with Marvin.

Leaving his cabin, he looked along the narrow path that led past the villa, and to the guardroom. Soon after

21.00, Marvin would release the dogs, and they would be on the prowl. When he had doped Marvin, Frost thought, he would have to leave his cabin around 02.00, walk along this path to the guardroom to neutralise the fence. The walk was roughly sixty yards. One or all the dogs could nail him before he reached the guardroom. He looked upwards. Could he reach the guardroom by climbing a tree, swinging himself on to the villa's roof and down to the guardroom? He dismissed this thought immediately. He was no Tarzan, and anyway, there were no overlapping trees. A problem!

He found Marvin watching the end of a ball game on the box.

'Hi, Mike.' Marvin got to his feet and turned off the set. 'Lousy game. Had a good day?'

'Swimming,' Frost said. 'I'm starved.' He pulled up a chair and sat at the table. 'No excitement?'

Marvin shook his head and sat opposite Frost.

'The excitement will start on Saturday. The Big Shot arrives.'

'So Old Creepy told me. Tell me about Grandi.' Frost offered his pack of cigarettes. As the two men lit up, he went on, 'How do you dig him?'

'You and I have handled dozens of thugs in our day,' Marvin said quietly. 'Grandi is yet another thug, but gold plated. Watch it with him. He likes playing God. Don't imagine because he gives you the big hello, he has taken a liking for you. I would rather deal with Old Creepy than Grandi. At least, you know Old Creepy is hostile. I've met Grandi twice, and twice is enough. I know because I'm an ex-cop, he hates cops. So watch it.'

At this moment, Suka came in with the dinner trays. He sat them down on the table, bowed and went away.

Frost looked at the thick pork chop with onions and french fried, and whistled.

'We certainly don't starve here. Tell me about Suka, Jack.' He began to cut into the chop. 'He never seems to stop working.' Frost was now probing for information. 'Does he sleep here?'

'Suka's special. He looks after us. Gina, Amando and the dogs. No, he doesn't sleep in the villa. He has a cabin around the back by the lagoon. He packs up around 23.00, and he starts work at 07.30. He's the only resident servant here. The rest of the staff leave before I release the dogs. They all live outside the estate.'

'There's no night staff then?'

'For what?' Marvin slapped mustard on his chop. 'The girl goes to bed around 22.00. Amando goes to his room around the same time. They don't need anything. But it's different when Grandi arrives. The whole staff are on duty until he goes to bed which is around 02.00. They love him! To get the staff home, I have to recall the dogs.' Marvin shrugged. 'He doesn't often come, and he doesn't stay long. He'll be off on Monday morning, and then everyone can relax.'

Frost now had some information, and knowing Marvin was an ex-cop, he decided it would be unsafe to probe further.

Then he felt a sudden cold chill run up his spine as he looked across the table at Marvin's relaxed, friendly face. This man was going to be murdered! Then he forced himself to think of the money he was going to pick up. Five million! Why the hell should he care about Marvin?

The food had become dry in his mouth. He forced himself to eat while his mind continued to be active.

'Have you got a girl, Jack?' he said, chewing hard.

'I've got something better than that,' Marvin said with an expansive grin. 'I've got a son.'

For the next ten minutes while they finished their dinner, Frost was subjected to a glowing eulogy of Marvin's son. According to Marvin, there had never been such a bright, smart phenomenon as Marvin junior. And as he listened, seeing the pride and happiness on Marvin's face, he knew now why Silk had said Marvin would co-operate.

'Who wants a woman when I'm so goddamn lucky to have a son like that?' Marvin concluded. 'I spend every hour when I'm off duty with him. I've got him well fixed. When the kid was born, my goddamn wife wouldn't take care of him. All she thought about was movies, farting around, having what she called a good time. So I hired an old black mamma, and she is great! She takes care of the kid. I wouldn't want for anyone better!'

'Yeah,' Frost said, pushing aside his plate. 'You're lucky. When you have a kid like that . . . '

'I know it.' Marvin got to his feet. 'Time I got rid of the staff and let the dogs loose.'

'You feed them, Jack?'

'Suka does it. He has a way with dogs. He's feeding them now.'

'Well, so long. Happy dreams.'

When Marvin had gone, Frost sat before the monitors. This day was Thursday. He had two more night duties. On Saturday, he would have to see Silk again. By Saturday, he would have to come up with the solution of his problems.

He heard Suka come in to collect the tray and he looked around.

'Fine meal, Suka,' he said.

The Japanese paused and regarded him, his face expressionless.

Frost studied him. Instinct warned him that this little man with his wooden face could be dangerous.

'I forgot to thank you for keeping guard, Suka,' he went on. 'You and I must try to keep Miss Gina happy.'

Suka inclined his head, stared for a long moment at Frost, and then left the room.

Frost grimaced, then shrugged, but again told himself that Suka could be yet another problem.

Now to see if he could solve his problems.

How was he going to dope Amando? This was the sixty-four thousand dollar question. The more he thought about it, the more complex the problem became. He had no information about Amando's habits. On the night that Gina was to be snatched, Amando might be away on a business trip: he might be at the villa: he might . . . God knew!

Frost rubbed his sweating jaw. A problem! He sat staring at the monitors and watched the dogs, sniffing around the trees. He thought of the moment when he would have to set off for the guardroom to neutralise the fence and he studied the dogs . . . all killers!

Hell! he thought, have I problems!

It wasn't until after midnight that an idea suddenly occurred to him. He did have some information about Amando, and he had forgotten about it up to this moment! His heart beating with excitement, he snatched up the telephone receiver and dialled the Spanish Bay hotel. In a minute or so, he was connected with Marcia.

'No talk, honey,' he said, keeping his voice low. 'Just say yes or no. Does Amando still come to you Saturdays?'

'Yes.'

'First Saturday in the month?'

'Yes.'

'What time?'

'Nine evening.'

'Does he take a drink?'

'Yes.'

'Okay, honey,' and Frost hung up.

The first problem solved!

Now the dogs.

He got to his feet and once again examined the control panel. He concentrated on the button that activated the silent whistle that recalled the dogs to their compound. If he could fix this, so when Marvin was doped, the whistle would get the dogs back into their compound, then the second problem would be solved. He knew nothing about electronics. He then remembered Umney had talked to the man who had fixed the alarm panel. Frost nodded to himself. Umney would have to talk to this guy again and find out how he (Frost) could fix the whistle button even if it meant twisting the guy's arm. Maybe this would be the second problem solved.

But how was he to dope Gina?

As he thought about this, he realised that she presented a dangerous problem. When she came out of sedation after her release, she must not have any suspicion that he had engineered her kidnapping. She was an unknown quantity to him, but he had an instinctive feeling that she would throw him to the cops if she had the slightest suspicion he had been behind her kidnapping.

Don't rush this, he told himself. I have until Saturday morning. At least, I reckon I have two of the problems fixed.

He switched his mind from Gina, and tried to relax, but then his mind switched to Marvin, doped, and at Silk's mercy. *You don't have to worry about Marvin. I'll take care of him.*

In his mind, Frost saw again Marvin's proud face as he had talked happily about his son. *Marvin will never be found.* Silk would murder him and hide his body. Silk was a professional. When he said the body would never be found, he meant just that.

Frost flinched and sweat beaded his forehead.

Drawing in a deep breath, he forced himself to relax.

Five million dollars! No more farting around, trying to scrape up a living! Five million, and the world was his!

Too bad about Marvin.

This was a once in a lifetime chance!

Five

The sound of the telephone bell brought Frost out of a heavy sleep. As he jerked upright, he looked at the wall clock. The time was 13.15. He grabbed up the telephone receiver.

'Mike?' Marvin's voice. 'Hustle into your uniform and come to the guardroom.' There was a note of urgency in his voice. 'Grandi's arrived, and it's action stations.' He hung up.

Grandi? Here? The fink was supposed to be arriving tomorrow!

Frost, cursing, rolled out of bed and went into the bathroom. In under fifteen minutes, he was shaved, showered and dressed, and he walked fast from his cabin to the guardroom.

He found Marvin waiting for him outside the guardroom door. Marvin gave him a crooked grin.

'Sorry about this, Mike,' he said. 'He crept up on us. Right now he is talking to Old Creepy. You stay here. I'm doing the patrol. Look busy.' He eyed Frost over. 'Watch it. He'll want to see you,' and he started off along the path leading to the lagoon.

Frost entered the guardroom and sat down. Through the open door, he saw the three Chinese gardeners were working with frantic haste. Usually, they plucked a weed, sneered at it, ruminated, then plucked another weed. Now, they were really sweating it out. Frost sensed an electrifying change in the atmosphere. Grandi had arrived!

As he sat before the TV monitors, he occasionally caught

a glimpse of Marvin, patrolling the estate. Marvin looked tense.

There came a tap on the door and Suka came in with coffee and two beef sandwiches.

'The boss is here,' he said, as he set down the tray. Frost thought even the unflappable Suka looked tense. 'You eat fast.'

But it wasn't until four hours later that Frost received his summons, and by then, he found he was also tense. Suka came into the guardroom.

'The boss wants you,' he said. 'Come with me, please.'

He led Frost to a room that led off the stairway to the upper floor. He stood aside and waved Frost forward.

The room was big with lounging chairs, a six-seater settee, a vast desk, a cocktail cabinet and occasional tables.

At the desk sat a squat, broad-shouldered man in his late fifties. He was wearing a T-shirt and bottle green slacks. His hairy, brown, muscular arms rested on the desk.

Marvin had described Grandi as a gold-plated thug. Looking at him as he approached the desk, Frost decided Marvin's description hit the nail squarely on the head.

The fat, swarthy evil-looking face with its small restless eyes, the short blunt nose, the thin lips, the high forehead, the shock of iron grey hair made a picture of ruthlessness, power and cruelty.

'Sit down!' Grandi snapped, and waved to a chair by his desk.

Frost sat down, sitting upright, his hands on his knees.

There was a pause while the two men regarded each other, then Grandi said, 'I have studied your dossier. You have worked for the F.B.I. While working with them, did you have a kidnap problem?'

'Yes, sir,' Frost said. 'I worked with others on the Lucas kidnapping.'

Grandi's eyes narrowed as he thought.

'Lucas? A girl? Yes . . . Lucas paid a million to get

90

her back. The snatchers were caught . . . right?'

'Correct, sir. Three of them were caught. The fourth got shot. I shot him.'

Grandi paused to study Frost. His restless eyes probed.

'Marvin has had no experience of kidnapping,' he said. 'What do you think of Marvin?'

Frost saw his chance, but he warned himself to play this one slow.

'Excuse me, sir, but I don't understand the question.'

Grandi shifted in his chair. His little eyes snapped.

'With your record, you can't be a fool.' His voice was a bark. 'I'm asking you your opinion of Marvin whose job is to protect my daughter. Don't prevaricate!'

Frost was sure Grandi had asked Marvin the same question about himself.

'Marvin is a dedicated ex-policeman, sir. He has a top class record. If I were in your place, I would have picked Marvin.'

Grandi nodded.

'He said the same about you, but he has never handled a kidnapping case, but you have. I believe in using men of experience. You have worked with the New York police and the F.B.I. It seems to me you have much more experience than Marvin has who has been just a State trooper. I am more interested in your opinions than Marvin's.' Again a pause while Frost looked directly at him. 'Very well, Frost, what do you think of the present security measures to protect my daughter from kidnapping?'

'Ninety-seven per cent perfect,' Frost said.

Grandi opened a box on the desk and took from it a cigar. He bit off the end, then lit it, puffing smoke at Frost.

'That leaves three per cent unsafe . . . according to you.'

'Yes, sir.'

Grandi leaned forward. His swarthy face ugly with scarcely controlled rage.

'Don't feed me this sort of shit!' he snarled. 'Is my daughter safe or isn't she?'

'As I see it, sir, there is a weak link in the security chain: the weak link is a possible inside man or woman,' Frost said quietly.

'I've thought of that. I talked to Chief of Police Terrell. He tells me all the staff working here have been screened, including yourself. Terrell is satisfied. He tells me there can be no inside man or woman.'

His expression wooden, Frost said, 'Then your daughter is one hundred per cent safe.'

Grandi shoved back his chair and walked across to the picture window. Looking at his squat figure, Frost saw this man was almost a midget. He couldn't have been more than five foot tall, but the power and the muscular build made him impressive.

Grandi swung around and pointed his cigar at Frost.

'You don't think so? You think there could be an inside man?'

'I said your daughter is ninety-seven per cent safe. I don't give a damn what Terrell thinks. There is a three per cent risk: small, but a risk.'

Grandi came back to his chair and sat down.

'So what's the three per cent risk? Spell it out.'

'If some smart operator kidnapped your daughter, he would demand at least fifteen million dollars ransom,' Frost said. 'Maybe to you, sir, fifteen million dollars aren't something you would risk your life or your freedom for, you are you, but there are millions of people who would risk their lives and their freedom for such money. So I am telling you, sir, that every man has his price. I am still saying that the weak link in the security chain, protecting your daughter, is a possible inside man.'

Grandi leaned forward, glared at Frost.

'What's your price, Frost? Would you be the inside man for fifteen million dollars?'

I'm going to be the inside man for five million dollars,

Frost thought. His police training was such that his expression remained wooden.

'I see your point, sir,' he said and got to his feet. 'You should ask yourself: if I was aiming to kidnap your daughter, why should I be talking like this? I'm telling you there is a remote possibility that there could be an inside man. It's part of my job to give you my opinion. It's up to you to take it or leave it. You've just asked me if I would act as an inside man for fifteen million. That's a fair question. I would not act as an inside man for thirty million dollars and I'll tell you for why.' He put both his hands on the desk and leaned forward to stare at Grandi. 'I don't sell out a client. If I'm hired to do a job, I do it. I'm cop trained, as Marvin is cop trained. Neither of us sell out a client. If you can't believe that, then I find myself another job. The ball is in your court,' and turning, he walked to the door.

'Frost!' The bark in Grandi's voice would have stopped a train. 'Come back here! Sit down!'

Frost then knew he had got over one big hurdle, but he also knew there were more hurdles ahead.

He walked back to the chair and sat down.

'This is the first constructive conversation I've had since I've come here,' Grandi said. 'I've talked to the Chief of Police, to Amando, to Marvin. They have all assured me my daughter is safe, now you tell me there is a three per cent risk. I want my daughter to be a hundred per cent safe. So, tell me about this three per cent risk . . .'

'The security here is top class,' said Frost. 'No one can get on this island without alerting Marvin and myself, and police headquarters. This has been well taken care of, and I can't fault it.' He paused, then went on, 'But if there was an inside man, the guardroom could be vulnerable. In this room are the controls. There are four men who have access to this room: Mr Amando, Suka, Marvin and myself. Mr Amando has the habit of checking to see if the night guard is asleep. He enters without warning. Suka brings in meals. To reduce the risk, sir, I suggest that Amando and Suka are no longer allowed into the guardroom. I said there was a three per cent risk. If Mr Amando and Suka are not allowed into the guardroom, the risk is cut to one per cent . . . a minute risk, but still a risk. If a kidnap attempt is made, the police and you will know that there are only two suspects: Marvin and myself. This narrows down the field. Both Marvin and I have been hired by you to protect your daughter. I can speak for him as I speak for myself: we don't sell out a client.'

Grandi nodded.

'I go along with your suggestions. I'll tell Amando and Suka to keep out of the guardroom. From now on, you and Marvin are responsible for my daughter's safety. Remember that!'

'Yes, sir.' Frost got to his feet. 'There is one more thing. I know I am speaking out of turn, but I think someone should say it. How long are you going to keep a young, healthy woman caged up in this villa? She is virtually a prisoner here. She . . . '

Grandi cut him short with a savage wave of his hand.

'You do your job, Frost!' he barked. 'When my daughter has learned to behave herself, she will be given more freedom. That's all!'

'Yes, sir.'

Frost found Marvin in the guardroom. Closing the door, he gave Marvin a detailed account of his interview with Grandi. Marvin listened, staring thoughtfully at Frost while he talked.

'So now,' Frost concluded, 'we have Amando off our backs. I had to bring Suka into it. I guess he can leave the food trays outside for one of us to collect.'

'You think there could be a risk . . . that some smart creep could get at the girl?' Marvin asked.

'No way,' Frost said. 'I was just getting Amando off our backs.'

Marvin rubbed his chin while he thought, then he grinned.

'Yeah. You did well, Mike. I've always said that creep spoilt the scene. Hats off to you for fixing him!'

'Let's hope he stays fixed.' Frost got to his feet. 'This is my day off. Do you want me to hang around? I itch for a swim.'

'You get off, but don't be late back.'

'See you. Any idea how long the big shot is staying?' Marvin grinned.

'I don't ask those kind of questions.'

Back in his cabin, Frost changed into slacks and a sweatshirt. He decided he would give Marcia a call. Maybe they could have another session together.

As he moved out of the cabin, he saw the Rolls driving down the drive with Amando at the wheel and Grandi at his side. Looking to his left, he saw Marvin leave the guardroom and start off towards the lagoon.

He paused, seeing in the distance, the three Chinese gardeners, now relaxed, lifting weeds and ruminating. Then from a clump of flowering shrubs, Gina appeared. Wearing stretched blue pants and a bra, she waved to him, then darted across the lawn towards him. Frost stepped back into the cabin as she joined him and he closed and locked the door.

They faced each other.

'Mike! I've got to talk to you,' she said breathlessly. 'You are the only one who can help me! You must help me!'

'I'll help you,' he said, smiling at her. 'What's the problem?'

'Don't be so goddamn glib!' she said, her voice shrill. 'Wait until you hear!'

Frost eyed her. Her face was drawn, she was shivering, little beads of sweat covered her forehead.

'Take it easy,' he said, his voice soothing. 'Sit down. Tell me.'

She dropped into a chair.

'You are the only one who can help me, Mike.' She beat her clenched fists on her knees. 'You've got to help me! You can have all the money in the world if you will help me.'

Frost pulled up a chair and sat by her.

'Tell me,' he said.

She stared at him, then took hold of his hand, her nails digging into his flesh.

'No one would believe this! My father is kinky! My father!' She jumped up and walked around the room, beating her fists together. 'Imagine! My father!'

Frost watched her, frowning. Was she high? he wondered. *You can have all the money in the world if you will help me.* Did she mean this? Was she being hysterical?

'Gina!' He put a snap in his voice. 'Quiet down. Tell me.'

She stood for a long moment, her eyes closed, then she came back and sat down beside him.

'My father is in love with me,' she said.

Frost stared at her.

'What's the problem? Fathers are supposed to love their daughters, aren't they?'

'Love!' Gina screamed at him. 'Are you so goddamn stupid you want me to spell it out? He doesn't love me the way fathers love their daughters! He's kinky. He's sick! He wants to screw me!'

Shocked, Frost gaped at her.

'That I can't believe,' he said.

'I'm telling you!' Again her voice was shrill. 'My mother killed herself! He didn't give a damn about her! It was me! You have only to watch him when he is with me! Don't you think I have enough experience of men to know? That's why he keeps away from me. He doesn't trust himself any more!'

Frost drew in a deep breath.

'For God's sake . . .'

'I had such a happy time in Rome. I knew the way he was, so I was so very careful. It never crossed his sick mind that I needed sex. Then those stupid creeps tried to kidnap me, and then all the publicity. Then my sick father realised what was going on.' Her face contorted as she fought back her tears. 'So he put me in this goddamn prison, and he'll keep me here so no man can enjoy me, and he'll keep me here until he is dead!'

Frost continued to gape at her. He could think of nothing to say.

'Mike! You must believe me! You are the only one who can help me!' She slid off the chair, and on to her knees, catching hold of Frost's wrists. 'I can't go on living like this! Listen, Mike, if he died, I would be free, and I would inherit all his money . . . billions of dollars!' Her nails dug into his wrists. 'Do you understand what I'm saying, Mike? You are the only one who can set me free!' She released his wrists, and falling forward between his knees, she rested her face against his chest. 'Mike! I am begging you to kill him.'

Frost sat for a long moment, motionless: his mind active.

He thought, Jesus! She's out of her mind! I don't believe a word she is saying! What the hell have I walked into?

'Mike!' Her fingers moved inside his shirt. 'You can have all the money in the world! Kill him for me! Free me! There's so much money, Mike. I don't care for money. All I want is freedom.'

To Frost, her fingers moving over his sweating chest, felt like spider's legs. Firmly and gently, he pushed her away, shoved back his chair and stood up, looking down at her as she knelt before him.

'Gina!' He put a snap in his voice. 'Pull yourself together! You can't mean you are asking me to kill your own father!'

She sat back on her heels, and he felt a chill run down his spine as he looked into her eyes. He was now sure she was reefer high.

'He is old, and utterly sick,' she said. 'I am young with my life before me. Kill him for me. Kill him and have whatever you want: all the money in the world.'

Frost moved away, turning his back on her. He had

been planning to kidnap her for five million dollars! He needed time to think about this sudden change of scene. Just suppose Grandi died? Would this half crazy girl really inherit her father's enormous fortune? Suppose she did? Frost felt his heartbeat quicken. His mind switched to Silk. He was a professional killer. He could wipe Grandi out without complications, but he wouldn't stay still once he knew he (Frost) could get all the money in the world from this girl.

This was something to think about.

Still, looking out of the window, his back to her, he said, 'How long will your father stay here?'

'A week.'

Well, in a week, he would have lots of time to think this thing out. He turned.

'I don't promise anything, baby,' he said, 'but you can hope.'

'When?' She got unsteadily to her feet.

'Soon. Let me think about it. I go on day duty on Sunday. Can you come here next Thursday night?'

She shook her head.

'Wednesday. My father and Amando are having a business conference with other men at nine. I can come then.'

'Then Wednesday?'

'Please, please free me, Mike,' then turning, she left the cabin.

Frost felt cold sweat run down his face. He stood at the window and watched her dart into the shrubs.

* * *

After two hours on the beach, and after a swim, Frost got in the T.R.7 and drove to the Ace of Spades. He arrived at 17.20, the graveyard time when the staff took time off, the parking lot was empty and activity was down to zero.

As he walked into the deserted restaurant, Ross Umney, sitting at a table, checking the lunch receipts, stood up.

'Hi, Mike!' His wide, charming smile was in evidence. 'Didn't expect to see you so early.'

'I've things to talk about,' Frost said curtly. 'Where's Silk?'

'Playing gin with Mitch. Let's go.'

Umney led Frost to the room above the swimming pool.

Silk and Goble were at the table by the big window. There was a side table by Goble's side containing cream buns and a big pot of tea. As Umney and Frost entered, Silk said, 'Gin,' and Goble threw down his cards, cursing.

Silk looked up, stared at Frost, and raised his eyebrows.

'Let's talk,' Frost said, and took a lounging chair away from the table.

'About what?' Silk gathered up the cards, looked at Goble, said, 'You owe me fifty bucks.'

'As if you would forget,' Goble said and stuffed a cream bun into his mouth.

'Let's talk,' Frost said impatiently. 'Cut the crap. We're in business, aren't we?'

Silk got to his feet, wandered over to an armchair near Frost and sat down.

'So?'

Goble reached for another cream bun, hesitated, then got up, and sat in a chair by Silk. Umney took the remaining chair.

'So, okay,' Frost said. 'I've got the problems fixed, so we snatch the girl.'

Silk smiled.

'That's good news.' He looked at Goble, then at Umney. 'I told you Mike was smart.'

'That's what you told us,' Goble said, his hard little eyes on Frost. 'So let's hear how smart he is.'

Silk turned to Frost.

'Go ahead. We want to know how you will dope Amando, Marvin and the girl. We want to know how you fix the dogs and neutralise the fence. Go ahead.'

. Frost lit a cigarette as he stared at Silk.

'You talk first. I'm telling you I have these problems fixed, but I'm not telling you until you tell me just how you guarantee me five million dollars. I don't go further until I know.'

Goble said, 'A real sonofabitch. I warned you, Lu.'

Frost moved swiftly out of his chair, caught hold of Goble's shirt front, heaved him to his feet, then giving him a violent shove, sent him staggering across the room.

'Call me that again, you fat slob,' Frost snarled in his cop voice, 'and I'll knock your teeth through the back of your larded neck!'

A gun jumped into Goble's hand.

'Mitch!' Silk's voice was quiet and deadly.

Goble glared at Frost, then put away the gun.

Silk went on, 'You spoke out of turn, Mitch.'

Goble hesitated, then nodded. He walked slowly back to his chair and sat down.

'I apologise, Mike,' he said.

Frost smiled at him.

'Fine. No problem,' and he sat down. Then he looked at Silk. 'Are we in business or do I walk out and forget the whole thing? I'm asking how you can guarantee – I repeat guarantee – that I get my rake off and it remains safe.'

'If I tell you that,' Silk said quietly, 'are you in with us?'

'I'm in with you if you convince me.'

'Don't rush it. I'll convince you, but once I've told you, there is no way out. You come in with us or I'll kill you.'

Unless I kill you first, Frost thought, his face expressionless. He said, 'You don't have to spell it out. You convince me my money is guaranteed, and I'm in.'

Silk nodded.

'Once we get the girl, this is the sweetest snatch you can imagine. There will be no blow back. Hear me? No possible blow back.'

Frost flicked ash off his cigarette.

'Come on! You are going to murder Marvin. The cops

here are smart. There is a chance of a blow back. Don't kid yourself that as soon as Grandi gets his daughter back, he won't turn on the heat.'

'Marvin doesn't get killed, and Grandi won't turn on the heat,' Silk said.

Frost stiffened, staring at Silk.

'That's why this snatch is so sweet,' Silk said. 'When I told you Marvin would disappear for good, I wanted to test your nerve. I wanted to be sure you would go along with a killing. There will be no killing, but I do know now that you would go along if there was a killing. That told me I had picked the right man. You can relax, Marvin will just be drugged.'

Frost slowly shook his head.

'Then the heat comes back to me. You said the heat would be on Marvin.'

'I said that, but it was a test. I wanted your reaction.' Silk leaned forward, his one eye glittering. 'There will be no heat . . . no heat at all. No cops . . . no nothing. The money will be paid, and the girl handed back. This I guarantee.'

Frost looked at Goble, then Umney, then back to Silk.

'Keep talking,' he said.

'I told you Ross can get information out of an oyster, and he can. When that flat-footed attempt was made to snatch the girl in Rome, I thought I would have a try. Mitch said no way after casing the security, but I kept thinking. So I sent Ross to Rome. He came up with information, but Mitch said no way because the girl was too well guarded. So I thought around and Marcia came up with you . . . the inside man. You tell me you have solved the problems of getting at the girl. I tell you, with your information, plus Ross's information, we have the sweetest snatch in the world.'

'What's Ross's information?' Frost asked.

Silk smiled his evil smile.

'So I tell you, but remember, once you know, you are in, and you stay in . . . right?'

'You are repeating yourself,' Frost said impatiently. 'What's the information?'

Silk studied him for a long moment.

'It can't be repeated too often. I want you to understand that once you know this information, you are with us, and there is no way out for you except a slug in your head . . . right?'

The two men studied each other. Silk's one eye looked lethal. Frost became aware he was sweating slightly.

Five million!

In a quiet, steady voice, he said, 'What information?' Silk continued to stare at him.

'Sure you want to know?' he asked in his deadly voice.

'Cut the crap, Silk!' Frost snapped. 'Go haunt someone else's house. You don't haunt mine!'

Silk smiled, then turned to Umney.

'Yes, go ahead, Ross. He's with us . . . tell him.'

'I got at Grandi's accountant: a guy named Guiseppe Vessi,' Umney said. 'He has a kink for young boys, and he has a wife with money. There was no problem to twist his arm. All the rich Italians are doing a tax evasion gimmick. For years, Grandi has been syphoning off some of his big profits into a numbered account in Switzerland. Vessi has been in charge of the operation. Right now, so Vessi tells me, the money hidden in Switzerland is around thirty million dollars. So I leaned on Vessi, and we came up with a deal. He gets ten million, and we get twenty million, and there is nothing Grandi can do about it. We have photocopies of all the Swiss transactions. If Grandi even considers turning on the heat when his daughter is snatched, with these photocopies given to the Italian tax creeps, he could go away in jail for fifteen years, and Grandi knows this. So, there is no problem, once we get the girl. We four – Lu, Mitch, you and I sign a document which will make us shareholders of five million each, and Grandi transfers the numbered account to us. We are all protected. There's no problem, and Vessi gets the balance.'

'But will Grandi transfer this account to us?' Frost

asked, a little bewildered by what he had heard.

'He either does and gets his daughter back, or he doesn't, and goes to jail for fifteen years. Can you imagine a man as rich as Grandi going to jail?' Umney asked, grinning.

'I told you, Mike, this is a sweet snatch,' Silk said. 'No cops: no trouble, but we have to get the girl. Now you tell us how.'

'I'd like to look at this document you're talking about, transferring the account to us,' Frost said.

'You don't take chances, do you?' Silk smiled evilly. 'Show him, Ross.'

Umney got up, crossed to a bureau, opened a drawer and returned with a sheet of paper which he gave Frost.

Frost studied what was written on the paper. At the bottom of the paper was space for Grandi's signature. He read again, then nodded.

'Yeah, I guess this buttons it up,' he said, and handed the paper back to Umney. 'Right. I'm satisfied. Now I'll take one problem at a time. Next Saturday night is D-day. If you don't want it that fast, we'll have to wait another month. Here's why: Marcia tells me she has a regular date with Amando every first Saturday of the month which is next Saturday. He arrives here around nine, takes a drink, performs and leaves. According to her this is a routine thing. You give her one of your pills and Amando is fixed. I forgot to ask you: do these pills dissolve fast and have they a taste?'

'Fast, and no taste,' Silk said.

'Okay, Amando takes the drink, and is knocked out by three in the morning. How do you like it so far?'

Silk nodded.

'No problem,' he said.

'Marvin and I always have dinner together,' Frost went on. 'We always have a couple of cans of beer so there is no problem slipping him a pill. I go on night duty on Sunday, so on this Saturday night, I tell him I'm tired and am going to bed. So he settles down to watch the monitors and around two in the morning, he is knocked out. So I've taken care of Amando and Marvin,' Frost paused, looking at Silk. 'You still with me?'

'You've fixed Amando and Marvin,' Silk said. 'Now, how about the dogs? How about the fence? How about doping the girl?'

'The girl won't need to be doped. She will fix the dogs and the fence,' Frost said.

Goble broke in angrily, 'Look, Lu, this guy is either conning us or else he's crazy in the head!'

Frost looked at him.

'I'm not taking any more from you, Fatso,' he said evenly. 'Flap with your mouth once more and I'll flatten you!'

'Shut up, Mitch!' Silk snarled. 'Keep out of this!' He turned to Frost. 'I'm listening . . . keep talking.'

'Grandi arrived at the villa this morning. He talked with me,' Frost then went on to give a detailed account of his interview with Grandi. 'So, I have got Amando and Suka off my back,' he concluded, 'and this is important. It means the guardroom is free of unexpected visitors. Now, here is the big news. Grandi and Amando took off this afternoon, and the girl came to my cabin. She is a real nut case. Can you guess what she begged me to do?' He paused, looking at the three men, then lowering his voice, he went on, 'She begged me to kill her father so she could be free.'

There was a heavy silence in the room, broken only by the sound of the air conditioner. Silk crossed and re-crossed his legs. Umney ran his fingers through his thick hair. Goble made a soft grunting noise.

'Probably, you three don't realise what it means to a girl of Gina's temperament to be shut up behind a lethal fence,' Frost said into the silence. 'This girl has hot pants. Her only out is for her father to die. She knows that. She knows as long as he lives, she will remain behind bars.' Frost paused to light another cigarette while the three men, sitting forward, stared at him, listening. 'Now I'll tell you something else. Grandi is kinky. I'm telling you what she told me, and she was pretty convincing. He has a thing for her – and I mean a thing – or should I spell it out? She knows. She's screwed around, and she knows men. When the Rome newspapers highlighted her way of life, Grandi put her behind bars. If he couldn't have her, no one else would. Are you getting the photo?'

'Keep talking,' Silk said. 'I'm with you so far.'

'As you assured me the ransom is guaranteed, I've based my thinking on this assurance. From what she told me, Gina will do anything, including having her father murdered, to get free. She and I have a date on Wednesday when Grandi will be out of the way. I intend to ask her how she would like to be kidnapped. In her neurotic state, I bet she will jump at the idea. I will explain I have three good friends who are willing to help her get her freedom, but we need her co-operation. She has direct access from the villa to the guardroom. All she has to do, I will tell her, is to enter the guardroom at 03.00 Sunday morning where she will find Marvin drugged. I will tell her the buttons to press and get the dogs out of the way to neutralise the fence. Then all she has to do is walk down to the harbour where you three will be waiting in a boat, and you will take her to a place of safety. I'm sure I can talk her into this, and you three don't even have to enter the grounds of the estate.' Frost looked inquiringly at Silk. 'Like it so far?'

'I like it so far. Keep talking.'

'Where will you keep her?'

'Here . . . where else? She can have Marcia's room.'

'That's fine. So we have the girl without trouble. The following morning I go to the guardroom to relieve Marvin, find him drugged, call Suka, find Amando drugged, and Gina missing. I find in the guardroom a sealed envelope on which is written: this is the ransom note to be handed to Grandi. No cops or else . . . So I take charge. I call Grandi. Suka will know where he will be. By the time Grandi arrives, Marvin and Amando will be back on their feet, but I will be very much in charge. Grandi reads the ransom note and sees he is stuck. He pays up or goes to jail. You give him a day to sweat it out, then you telephone, and with luck, he agrees to meet one of you. I'll be right on the scene to check he doesn't try anything smart. He knows I've handled a kidnap before when I was with the Feds so he will consult me. So he takes me along with him to complete the deal. You get the signed document and hand over the girl, then you fade from the scene. That leaves Gina, Grandi and me. She will tell her father to go screw himself. I will tell him he can't legally hold her, so Gina goes off. I couldn't care less where she goes, but the deal will be that she goes. I go back to the villa with Grandi. Once he realises he has lost his daughter, he will close up the villa and pay Marvin and me off. So I take a fast plane to Switzerland, collect my share of the loot and live happily ever after.' Frost smiled at Silk. 'What do you think?'

Silk nodded.

'It's smart, Mike.' He looked at the other two. 'What do you say?'

'I like it,' Umney said. 'Yeah, it's smart.'

Goble got to his feet and helped himself to the last cream bun on the tray.

'I see problems,' he said, biting into the bun. 'Let's talk the whole thing out, huh?'

So the four men sat around the table and talked it out. An hour later, Frost shoved back his chair and stood up.

'I've got to get back,' he said. 'You're all satisfied, providing I can talk sense into Gina?'

'That's it,' Silk said. 'You convince us she'll play, then the deal's on.'

'I'll be here Thursday evening at 18.00,' Frost said. 'I'll want a copy of this document, signed by you three. I want a copy of the ransom note for Grandi.'

'Okay,' Silk said. 'Looks like we're in business, Mike.'

Nodding to the three of them, Frost left the room.

There was a long silence, then Mitch got up and opened

the door and looked up and down the empty corridor. He closed the door and leaned against it.

'I trust that creep the way I would trust a rattlesnake.'

'Don't worry about him,' Silk said with his evil smile. 'Rattlesnakes are expendable, aren't they?'

* * *

Wednesday evening: 21.00 hrs.

Frost moved around his cabin restlessly. Every now and then, he slammed his clenched fists together. He had seen Grandi and Amando drive away in the Rolls soon after 20.00. He had picked at a good dinner, then telling Marvin he was bushed, he left him before the monitors and had gone to his cabin. Marvin had warned him he would release the dogs at exactly 21.00.

As the hands of his watch moved to 21.03, he snapped off the light and moved to the window.

God! he thought, how the past five days had dragged! Being on night guard, he had seen nothing of Grandi. He had spent the days on the beach. He hadn't been near the Ace of Spades. Now, at last, Wednesday had arrived, but he still wasn't sure if Gina would come to him. What a fiasco it would be if she didn't! Then he saw her dart out of the shrubs and come racing towards his cabin. He had the door open as she arrived. She threw herself into his arms, her body straining against his, and he had to push her away to shut and lock the door, then he caught hold of her.

'Oh, Mike . . . I've been waiting and waiting!' she exclaimed. 'Every hour of these awful days has tormented me!'

He swung her off her feet and carried her into the bedroom. He paused to switch on the bedside light, then lowered her on to the bed. He had previously drawn the curtains, and he knew Marvin, from the guardroom, couldn't see the light in the bedroom.

'I've been waiting too,' he said, leaning over her. 'How long have we got?'

'Three hours . . . not more.'

She was already wriggling out of her stretch pants, and he pulled them free as she unstrapped her bra.

Their coupling was ferocious: two uninhibited animals, and when she finally reached the top of the crest, she gave a strangled, suppressed scream.

They lay in each other's arms while their breathing quietened. Frost held her gently, but he was now aware of the passing minutes.

'Gina, honey,' he said, still holding her, 'I think I have found a way out for you.'

He felt her stiffen against him. She pushed away from him and sat up.

'You mean you will kill him?'

Looking at her, seeing how her eyes glittered, Frost felt chilled. She must be crazy in the head! he thought. Play this very, very softly.

'No . . . I have a better idea. You see, honey, if I killed him, the cops would come into it, and where would I be then?'

'You're smart!' She caught hold of his arm. 'You'll find a way to make it look like an accident.' Her grip tightened. 'Think! If he was dead, you would have all the money in the world!'

'How do you know for sure he'll leave his money to you?' Frost asked.

'Who else is there but me?' She smiled as her fingers began to caress his arm. 'I'll be richer than Christina Onassis! Billions of dollars! You can have as much as you want. Kill him, Mike, and I promise you the earth!'

Frost looked away. He didn't want her to see his revulsion.

'No, I've a better idea: no complications: no risk, no cops, and you get your freedom.'

She regarded him, her head a little on one side. He thought how corrupt and vicious she looked.

'What idea? What idea is better than killing this kinky old creep?'

This is it, he thought. If she doesn't fall for it, then what the hell am I to do?

Looking directly at her, he said slowly and distinctly, 'How would you like to be kidnapped?'

Her eyes widened, then she laughed gleefully.

'Kidnapped! I'd love it! I've always wanted to be kidnapped! When those jerks in Rome tried to kidnap me, I was so excited, I wet myself. Will you kidnap me, Mike? I'd love to be put in a cupboard like Patty Hearst. I would love to be treated rough. I would love to be raped!'

Listening to her, looking at her, Frost felt sick. He rolled off the bed and stood away from her. As he pulled on his jeans, she dropped flat on her back, her nipples hard, her legs widespread.

'Don't do that,' she said. 'I love to see you naked.'

Ignoring her, Frost went over to the dressing table where he had put a bottle of Scotch and glasses. He poured himself a stiff shot, then looked at her.

'A drink?'

She grimaced.

'No . . . come here. Tell me about this kidnapping.'

He emptied the glass at a swallow, then lit a cigarette, and came over to the bed. He sat at the end of it, away from her.

'This is a smart idea,' he said, 'but first I want to get the record straight. You told me you don't give a damn about money. Are you still telling me that?'

She regarded him, then nodded.

'There is only one thing I care about,' she said. 'I want to be free and do my thing. I don't give a shit about money. I just want to take off and do my thing.'

'If you really mean that, I have the answer.'

'I mean it. Tell me.'

'I can fix it for you to be kidnapped. I have friends who will co-operate.'

'Who?'

'You don't need to know, honey, but I assure you, you don't have to worry about them.'

Her eyes probed.

'What do they get out of it?'

'The ransom.'

'And what do you get out of it?'

'Some of the ransom.'

'So, fill me in.'

He wasn't sure if he had hooked her, but he now knew he had to give her the plan. For the next half hour, he talked persuasively. He explained what she would have to do. He explained about the tax evasion money.

'He can't do a thing without going to jail, honey. You get your freedom, I get the ransom. Between us, we have him over a barrel,' he concluded. He paused, aware he was sweating. 'How does it look to you?'

Her hands stroked her breasts, and she smiled at him.

'Marvellous . . . wonderful!'

He regarded her uneasily.

'Sure?'

'Of course, I'm sure. So Saturday . . . I'll be free!' She slid down the bed and pulled him to her. 'No more talk, Mike . . . let's have some action!'

Six

Frost had just finished dressing when Suka came to the cabin.

Frost had slept badly. Although Gina had seemingly agreed excitedly to the idea of her being kidnapped, she worried him. He was almost sure that she was reefer smoking, and had been high the previous night. Suppose when she sobered up, she had a change of mind? He had rehearsed over and over again what she had to do.

At exactly three o'clock on Sunday morning, she was to go to the guardroom. There she would find Marvin drugged. She was to press the red button on the third row on the panel and wait for at least ten minutes. Then she was to press the fourth button in the same row. She was then to go straight to the harbour where she would find a boat waiting for her.

'Marvellous! Wonderful! Exciting!' she had said, and repeated what he had said, but he kept wondering if she would remember to press the right buttons. If she pressed a wrong button, every cop in Paradise City would be arriving. The thought made him sweat.

As Suka tapped, then peered into the cabin, Frost scowled at him.

'What do you want?' he demanded aggressively.

'Mr Grandi asks for you,' Suka said. 'Please to come with me.'

Alert, Frost followed him along the path and into the

111

villa. Suka conducted him into the room where Frost had met Grandi before.

Grandi was behind his desk. Standing by the window, his hands behind his back, was Amando.

Frost paused in the doorway, aware that Suka had faded away.

'Come in, Frost,' Grandi said.

Frost moved up to the big desk while Grandi stared up at him.

'I am leaving now,' Grandi said. 'I've talked to Marvin. From now on, Frost, you are in charge. Marvin will do what you say. Understand?'

'If you say so, sir,' Frost said, startled.

'That's what I'm saying. You have more experience than he has. This has been explained to him. From now on you get nine hundred dollars a week.'

'Thank you, sir,' Frost said, stiffly.

Grandi leaned forward, his stubby finger pointing at Frost.

'You'll earn it! My daughter is to remain here! If anything goes wrong, I'll make you wish you were dead! Understand?'

Frost looked into the ruthless, evil little eyes and felt himself flinch.

'Yes, sir.' He paused, then went on, 'I told you . . . '

Grandi cut him short with a wave of his hand.

'I know what you told me. My daughter stays here! Do you understand?'

Frost drew in a deep breath.

'Yes, sir.'

Grandi swung around to Amando.

'You hear what he said?'

'Yes, Mr Grandi.'

'Right,' Grandi made a gesture of dismissal.

'Excuse me, sir,' Frost said, 'but as I am in charge now, I want to know where I can contact you.'

Grandi leaned back in his chair, staring at Frost.

'Why?'

Frost wanted to lick his dry lips, but he stopped in time.
'In case of any emergency, sir.'

'What emergency?' The ruthless eyes bored into Frost.
Suddenly, Frost lost his fears of this squat tycoon.

'How the hell do I know?' he snarled in his cop voice.
'Anything can happen! If you want to stay out of sight,
it's your funeral, but if this guy, Amando, walks under a
truck, if Marvin falls into the lagoon, if I break my goddamn neck somehow, this, to me, is an emergency. You
following me, Mr Grandi?'

Grandi relaxed.

'You have made your point, Frost.' He scribbled on a
scratch pad, tore off the sheet and shoved it across the
desk. 'Any time, you can reach me.'

Frost took the sheet, stepped back, and said, 'Thank
you, sir.'

'I'm relying on you,' Grandi said.

'That you can do, sir,' Frost said, then he walked out
of the room, and shut the door behind him.

An hour later, back in his cabin, Frost watched,
through the big window, Grandi drive away in the Rolls.

He then walked to the guardroom where he found
Marvin.

'Hi, boss,' Marvin said as Frost walked in.

'Cut it out, Jack,' Frost said. 'We're both in this racket.
Don't blame me for Grandi's ideas. We're here to make
a living. I'm no more boss than you.'

Marvin grinned wryly.

'Yeah . . . so let's earn a living. So you're in charge now.
Do you have any extra ideas?'

'The setup is sweet to me. I'm going for a swim. Remember? It's my day off.'

'You think about it, Mike. Maybe you could have ideas.'

Frost walked up to him and gave him a playful thump
on his chest.

'We're organised, Jack. No problem. This fink's just
shooting off with his mouth.'

Marvin relaxed.

'When dealing with a thug like him, anything can happen. Okay, Mike, we work together.'

Although his date with Silk was at 18.00, Frost decided there was no point in waiting, so when he left Marvin, he drove to the Ace of Spades, arriving there a little after 14.20.

The restaurant was crowded, but Umney, moving around, showing his teeth at the clients, saw Frost as he came in, and he came quickly to his side.

'Where's Silk?' Frost demanded.

'He's busy,' Umney said, 'but he'll be free in half an hour. How about some lunch, Mike?'

'Where's Marcia?'

'On her back. I haven't eaten yet. Let's you and me have a lobster salad . . . right?'

Frost found he was hungry.

'Okay.'

Umney led him to a side room. A waiter materialised. 'A drink?'

'Sure . . . gin on the rocks.' Frost sat at the table, and looked around. In a corner, two girls were eating. One was wearing black slacks and was topless; her tiny breasts were like poached eggs. Her companion was lush, blonde and stupid-looking. On the far side of the room was a fat, elderly man caressing the hand of a blond boy who was giggling.

As the waiter brought the drinks, Frost said, 'Nice people you have here.'

'Turds, but they have the money,' Umney said indifferently, 'and we are all after the money.'

'You can say that again,' Frost said.

The lobster salad was served.

As they began to eat, Umney said, 'You got it fixed, Mike?'

'I've got it fixed,' Frost said.

Umney forked lobster into his mouth.

'Lu will be glad to hear the news.'

'Rest your mouth, Ross, I'm eating,' Frost said.

They finished lunch in silence, then Frost pushed back his chair.

'Go find Silk,' he said.

Umney found Silk in the shooting range. Silk had just won three thousand dollars off a playboy who thought he was the best shot in the city until he had challenged Silk.

'Frost's here,' Umney said. 'He says he's fixed it. He's acting tough.'

'They all act tough,' Silk said, handing his pistol to Moses. 'Let's see what he has come up with. Where's Mitch?'

'Stuffing his gut . . . where else?'

Five minutes later, Frost, Silk, Umney and Goble were sitting around the table in the room overlooking the swimming pool.

The three men listened while Frost talked.

'So it's on,' Frost concluded. 'I could have a slight problem with the girl. She's a reefer smoker. She wants to be kidnapped. Could be, at the last moment, she'll change her mind. This is a risk we'll have to take.'

'So long as she neutralises the fence so we can get in,' Silk said, 'she can change her goddamn mind as often as she likes.'

'Now I want the pill for Marvin,' Frost said.

Silk produced a tiny pill box.

'All you have to do is drop it in his drink. Within six hours, he won't know what's hit him.'

'For how long?'

'Guaranteed for seven hours.'

'So, I dope this drink at eight o'clock and he gets knocked out at two o'clock, and he surfaces at nine . . . right?'

'That's guaranteed.'

'And Amando?'

'Marcia will fix him. He'll come to the surface around the same time.'

'So, okay, let's get down to the paperwork. I want to see the ransom note.'

Umney opened a briefcase and took from it a sheet of paper.

'Here it is . . . it's a draft, but if you want it changed, we'll try again.'

The ransom note was brief:

Sign the enclosed order to the National Bank, Lugano. You will be given instructions by telephone how to deliver this order to us. Any tricks, and you will not only go to jail for tax evasion (specimen copies of your tax frauds enclosed) but you will not see your daughter again.

Frost nodded.

'Okay. Now how about the order to the bank he has to sign?'

Umney produced another paper. This was a letter to be signed by Grandi to the National Bank, Lugano, instructing them to transfer thirty million dollars from account No. G/556007 to account No. N/88073, Ferandi Bank, Zurich.

Frost looked at Silk.

'What's this 88073 account?'

'For years, I have had a numbered account with Ferandi,' Silk said quietly. 'They know me, so there is no problem paying in thirty million. It's a private bank and they deal with people who want to sweep money under the carpet: tax evasion, Presidents who don't think they will last long, film stars . . . no problem.'

'So the money goes into your own personal numbered account?'

'There's no way else to do it, but we're all covered.' Silk nodded to Umney who produced another paper.

Frost studied it. This was an order to Ferandi Bank to pay to each of the signatures (on production of passports) the sum of five million dollars drawn from the thirty million dollars of account G/556007, National Bank, Lugano, and to pay from this account the sum of ten million dollars to Mr Guiseppe Vessi at his request.

'We all sign,' Umney said, 'and each has a copy. When we have the girl, I telephone Grandi. I arrange to meet him at the Three Square motel which is a good meeting place with plenty of cover. Lu and Mitch will be there, out of sight.' He paused, then went on, 'He can't afford to be tricky, but we have you as an inside man. If you think he's calling the cops or acting smart, you'll alert me. I have a gimmick here,' he took from the briefcase a small, flat box. 'This is a bleeper. You have this, I have another. If you think Grandi is going to act smart, all you have to do is to press this little button and my bleeper is activated, and the operation is cancelled, but to my thinking, he can't afford to be tricky.'

'Okay,' Frost said. 'So you have the signed banker's order. What happens then?'

'Lu flies to Zurich and checks the transfer. He gives me the green light when the money has arrived. Then we release the girl. Then when the smoke's died down, say in a week, we three fly out and join Lu. We each take our share and split up. How do you like it?'

Frost sat still while he thought, then turned to Silk.

'What happens if one of us dies?'

Silk's face turned wooden.

'Who's talking about dying?'

'I am,' Frost said, then leaning forward, staring at Silk, he went on, 'I want life insurance. There's nothing to stop any of you three putting a bullet in me as soon as you have the banker's order. I'm not signing anything unless there's a clause put in this agreement. I either get it or the deal's off.'

'What clause?' Silk asked.

'If within one month from the date of Grandi's order, any one of us doesn't claim his share, his share goes anonymously to Oxfam.' Frost smiled at Silk. 'Don't think I'm being charitable. It means it won't be worth your while or your risk to kill me, and it won't be worth my while or risk to kill you three. Get the idea?'

Silk laughed.

'Okay.' He looked at Umney. 'Fix it the way he wants it, Ross.'

Umney shrugged, then grinned at Frost.

'I'm getting the idea, Mike, you don't trust any of us.'

'You can say that again,' Frost said, then getting to his feet, he went on, 'I'm taking a swim. I'll be back in an hour. Have it fixed by then.'

When he had gone, Goble said, 'I warned you he is a smart sonofabitch, Lu.'

'He's looking after himself,' Silk said, and smiled his evil smile.

*　　*　　*

Before returning to the Grandi estate, Frost stopped off at the National Florida Bank and lodged his copy of the agreement in a safe deposit box. He was now reasonably sure that he had covered himself, but he was taking no chances. When dealing with a thug like Silk, one thoughtless slip could be the last.

Two more days to D-Day! he thought as he let himself into his cabin. Everything now depended on Gina. If she changed her mind, if she pressed the wrong button . . . ! He wondered what she was doing right now. As he had driven up to the villa, he had seen Amando, at a table, covered with papers, on the terrace, but there had been no sign of Gina.

He changed into his uniform, then later, walked to the guardroom. The time was now 19.75, and he found Marvin, relaxed, before the monitors.

'Had a good day, Mike?' Marvin asked, turning.

'Building up my tan.' Frost sat down by his side. 'Any excitements?'

'She's sick,' Marvin said, lighting a cigarette.

Frost stiffened.

'Come again?'

'I didn't see her around so I asked Old Creepy. He said she was in bed, and not to worry.'

Jesus! Frost thought. It only wants this!

'Something bad?'

Marvin shrugged indifferently.

'You know girls . . . they have troubles. There's been no doctor, so I guess it's the usual thing.'

'Who the hell would want to be a girl?' Frost said, drawing in a deep breath.

'Yeah. Anyway, I didn't have to keep my eye on her.' Marvin flicked ash, then went on, 'You know something? Strictly between ourselves, I think the girl's not right in her head. I think she's as nutty as a fruit cake.'

Frost became very alert.

'What makes you say that, Jack?'

'I've seen a lot more of her than you have,' Marvin said. 'She doesn't act like a normal girl. There's something about her that really bothers me . . . spooky could be the word.'

Frost thought of Gina's glittering eyes, the touch of her fingers, her wish that her father was dead. Spooky, he thought, was a good word.

'You can't expect any girl living like a caged animal to be normal,' he said.

'There's that.' Marvin rubbed his jaw, then shrugged. 'She asked me to give her a gun.'

Frost stared at him.

'A gun?'

'She said she would feel safer to have a gun. She told me she was scared of Old Creepy. She said when she was alone with him, she felt he wanted to rape her.'

'It would scare me to have Old Creepy continually around me. So what did you tell her?'

'I told her no way, and that either you or I were always around so she had nothing to be scared about.'

Just then there came a tap on the door, signalling to them their dinner had arrived. Suka, following Grandi's instructions, no longer came into the guardroom.

Frost got to his feet, unlocked the door and stepped into the dimly lit hall in time to see Suka walking away. He brought in the two trays.

'Looks good,' he said, setting down the trays. 'I'll get the beers.'

He went to the refrigerator, took out two cans, opened them with his back turned to Marvin. Saturday night, he reminded himself, he would repeat the performance, but into Marvin's can, he would drop the pill Silk had given him.

'I'm damn grateful I've got a boy,' Marvin said, as they began to eat. 'On Sunday, I'm taking him to the funfair. He's crazy about riding the dodgems.'

During the meal, Marvin talked on about his son while Frost half listened, then when Marvin had gone, Frost settled down before the monitors. He watched the dogs being released. This was routine, his mind was on Gina.

Around midnight, still worrying about Gina, he went to the door leading to the villa, unlocked it and edged it open. The hall was in darkness. He stood listening, then hearing no sound, he took from his hip pocket a small flashlight, stepped into the hall and closed the door behind him. He was aware of the risk he was taking. If Amando caught him, the operation would be blown, but the urge to check on Gina, to make sure she wasn't really ill, to once again check she still wanted to be kidnapped, compelled him forward.

Moving fast, cat-like, silently, he climbed the stairs, paused at the head of them, listened, then went quickly to Gina's room. He turned the handle, pressed and the door yielded. As it opened, he saw there was a faint light. Moving fast, he entered the room and closed the door.

Gina, a dim bedside light illuminating her, was lying in bed. She started up, staring at him, then her face, half in shadow, lit up.

'Mike!' she whispered, sat up and stretched out her arms to him. 'I've been waiting and waiting.'

He came to the bed, catching hold of her hands.

'Are you all right?' he asked. 'Marvin said you were sick.'

She giggled: a sound that made Frost's nerves creep.

'I'm fine. I didn't want to see the kinky old creep again so I took to my bed.' Her fingers moved along his arms. 'Let's make love. Mike! I have this thing for you. I've been waiting and waiting.'

Why did her dry fingers remind him of the feel of spider's legs? He swept aside her hands, looking at her. Yes . . . as Marvin had said . . . spooky was the right word.

'No way,' he said, his voice low and harsh. 'Listen, baby, it's all fixed. I'm taking a hell of a risk, but I had to have a word with you. When I heard you had gone sick, I was scared. You remember what you have to do, and you'll be free.'

Her hands moved along his trouser legs, but again he swept them away.

'Gina! Later. We'll have all the loving you'll ever need, but I must get back to the guardroom. You really remember what you have to do?'

She dropped back on her pillow and made a grimace.

'Of course I do. Three o'clock on Sunday morning, I go to the guardroom, press the red button on the third row of the panel. This recalls the dogs. I wait ten minutes, then press the fourth button on the same row. Then I go down to the harbour where your friends are waiting . . . right?'

'That's it.' Frost got to his feet and forced a smile. 'Do all that, and you'll be free to live your thing.'

He moved to the door, waved to her, eased open the door, looked into the dark corridor, then made his way silently back to the guardroom.

As he settled before the monitors, he told himself he had taken every possible precaution. The operation, which would make him five million dollars, was now in the lap of the gods.

* * *

Friday and Saturday dragged by.

Frost kept clear of the Ace of Spades. He spent the

long hours on the beach. His mind concentrated on what five million dollars would mean to him. Every so often some dolly in a skimpy bikini came over to him and asked if he was lonely. He waved them away. There would be time, when he got the money, to think about dolly birds.

Saturday night finally arrived.

This was it, he thought as he walked to the guardhouse. He had the pill for Marvin. He had telephoned Marcia who told him Amando was keeping his usual appointment at 21.00, and she would slip him the pill.

Frost found Marvin in the guardroom.

'Had a good day?'

The routine question.

'Fine . . . and you?'

'She's up and about. No problems.'

Frost went to the refrigerator.

'I've got a thirst. Join me?'

'Whoever refuses beer?'

Frost got two cans from the refrigerator, turned his back on Marvin, opened the cans and dropped the pill into one of them. He poured the drinks into glasses, then gave Marvin the doped glass. They drank. Marvin sighed, 'Tomorrow I see my son.'

Tomorrow, Frost thought as he drank, all hell will break loose.

They talked, then there came a tap on the door.

'Dinner time,' Frost said, and went to the door. He carried in the two trays.

As they began to eat, Marvin said, 'The day's stint is easy, Mike. All you have to do is walk around and look busy. Old Creepy will be watching you. Keep away from Gina. Don't talk to her. Just keep walking around.'

'Sure.' Frost finished the meal, then pushed back his chair. 'I'm having an early night. See you tomorrow at eight . . . okay?'

Marvin grinned at him.

'Don't be late. I want a few hours sleep. I'm picking my son up at midday.'

'I'll be here,' Frost said, then walked to his cabin. He set his alarm clock to go off at 01.00, then slipping out of his uniform, he stretched out on the bed and turned off the light, but he didn't sleep.

The hours crept by. Nine – ten – eleven – midnight. Impatiently, he turned on the light, then sat up. Another three hours! He found he was sweating. Getting off the bed he took a cold shower. What was Gina doing? He was still uneasy about her. Drying himself, he felt the pressure. Suppose she blew her cork? He remembered what Marvin had said: *she's as nutty as a fruit cake*. He grimaced, shrugging. There was nothing he could do now. He had to hope.

He put on slacks and a black shirt, then he turned off the light and sat by the window. He saw one of the dogs go by. He sat there, from time to time, looking at his strap watch. The hands crawled around to 02.00, moved on while Frost sat motionless. By now, if he could rely on Silk, Marvin was knocked out. Amando too should be knocked out. He wiped the sweat off his face with the back of his hand. Suppose Gina had fallen asleep? There was nothing he could do, except wait.

So he waited. Then when the hands of his watch crawled to three, he stood up. If Gina hadn't chickened out, she would be now leaving her bedroom, making her way down the stairs to the guardroom. She would first press the button that released the silent dog whistle. It would take some ten minutes before the dogs returned to their compound.

Frost remained at the window, his heart thumping, his mouth dry. Then, after an interminable wait of ten minutes, he pulled his gun from its holster and stepped out into the hot, humid air.

He began a slow, cautious, silent walk towards the guardroom, his eyes searching the darkness, ready to shoot if one of the dogs pounced on him. He reached the guardroom without incident.

Drawing in a deep breath of relief, he opened the guardroom door and moved in.

The room was lit. The shady light from the monitors made square puddles. Marvin lay, sprawled back in one of the chairs.

Frost took him in with a glance, then he looked at the alarm panel. The red button recalling the dogs was alight. Further along, the other red button that neutralised the fence was also alight.

So she had remembered and she had done it!

Frost bent over Marvin, looked carefully at him, then nodded. The pill had worked!

He stood motionless, thinking of Gina who by now must have reached the harbour. She would find the boat waiting for her.

Frost wiped the sweat off his face.

The first stage of the operation had worked!

* * *

Umney steered the motorboat towards the Grandi harbour. Goble sat in the bow. The time now was 03.17. The lagoon was in darkness.

'More to your right,' Goble said, 'take it dead slow.'

Umney cut the engine and the boat drifted forward.

Both men were tense. Silk had left the job to them.

'Collect her and bring her back here,' he had ordered.

Goble turned on the powerful flashlight he was holding.

'There she is! Let's go!'

The boat surged forward as Umney opened up. Still keeping the beam of the light on the harbour, both men could see Gina standing on the harbour arm.

She waved to them as the boat came alongside.

'Hi, there!' she exclaimed. 'Are you Mike's friends?'

'That's right, Miss Grandi,' Umney said. He had been warned by Silk to give her the V.I.P. treatment. 'Hold a moment.'

Leaving Goble to secure the boat, he clambered on to the harbour wall by her side.

'No problems, Miss Grandi?'

She released a giggle.

'Absolutely super. I have things with me.'

By her was a big suitcase and an air travel bag.

'I'll take care of them,' Umney said, and passed the items of luggage down to Goble.

'Where are we going?' Gina asked.

'We have everything fixed for you, Miss Grandi,' Umney said. 'Let me help you.'

She looked down at the boat, then moved to him, leaning against him.

'I don't want to fall in.'

Umney felt her fingers move on his body. She giggled again.

'You're quite a man,' she said.

He swung her off her feet and lowered her into the boat which Goble steadied.

What the hell have I got here? he thought, but the feel of her fingers excited him.

Climbing by her, he revved up the engine and backed the boat out of the harbour.

Gina regarded Goble in the semi-darkness. Her fingers touched his fat larded shoulder, and she drew away.

'You eat too much,' she said, and joined Umney.

Umney laughed as she sat by his side and pressed herself against him.

*　　*　　*

At 07.30, Frost, who hadn't slept, put on his uniform. He had shaved carefully, had showered, but looking in the mirror as he was shaving, he saw his face was tight drawn, and there were black shadows under his eyes. He waited until 07.50, then leaving his cabin, he walked to the guard-room. He knew that at exactly 08.00, Suka would bring the breakfast trays. He would tap on the door and go away.

Frost entered the guardroom.

Marvin lay, slumped in the lounging chair, snoring and breathing heavily.

Frost acted out his part. He pulled Marvin upright, shook him, then let him drop back in the chair, as he did so there came a tap on the door.

Suka!

Bracing himself, Frost opened the door.

Suka was moving off.

'Suka!' Frost snapped. 'Marvin's ill or something. Take a look at him!'

Suka paused, turned to stare at Frost, then moving by him, he entered the guardroom. He bent over Marvin, shook him, then looked up, his face expressionless.

'Drugged.'

Still acting out his part, Frost swung around and stared at the alarm panel.

'The fence has been neutralised!' he exclaimed. 'Check on Miss Grandi! I'll alert Amando. Where do I find him?'

'I do it,' Suka said, and moving rapidly, he rushed up the stairs.

Frost stood at the bottom of the stairs, waiting. He looked at his strap watch. The time was now 08.05. In another five minutes, Silk would telephone.

Suka appeared at the head of the staircase.

'Miss Gina not here! Mr Amando drugged!'

'Search the house!' Frost said. 'Make sure she isn't here!'

As Suka came down the stairs, the telephone bell in the guardroom began ringing.

'Hold it!' Frost said. He beckoned to Suka. 'This could be trouble. I want you to hear. Use the extension!'

As Suka picked up the extension receiver, Frost snatched up the other receiver.

'Yes?'

'Tell Grandi this is a snatch.' Frost guessed Silk was talking behind a handkerchief, but his voice still sounded menacing. 'We have his daughter. We'll call again tomorrow at this time. Tell him no cops,' and the line went dead.

As Frost replaced the receiver, he looked at Suka who was staring at him.

'Could be a hoax,' he said. 'Check the house. Make sure she isn't around.'

'No hoax,' Suka said, his little black eyes showing alarm. 'Better call Mr Grandi.'

Frost snatched up the telephone and called the guard on the barrier at the estate's entrance. He told him no one was to leave the estate and when the staff arrived they were to be told to take the day off.

'No one leaves without my permission,' he said.

'You got trouble up there?' the guard demanded.

'Nothing we can't handle,' Frost said curtly. 'Just follow instructions.' He hung up, then seeing Suka still hovering in the doorway, he waved him away.

'Check the house!'

He waited until Suka had gone, then taking from his shirt pocket the New York telephone number Grandi had given him he dialled. As he was waiting for the connection, Marvin moaned, then slowly sat up. He pressed his hands to his eyes.

A voice said from New York, 'Mr Grandi's residence.'

Frost could imagine a prim faced, black butler at the other end of the line.

'I must talk to Mr Grandi,' Frost said. 'Tell him Frost calling from Orchid Villa. This is an emergency.'

'Yes, sir.'

There was a long pause.

Marvin shook his head, then stared at Frost, his eyes glazed.

'What the hell goes on?' he muttered.

Frost waved him to silence as Grandi came on the line.

'What is it, Frost?' The snarl in Grandi's voice was chilling.

'Miss Grandi has been kidnapped, sir,' Frost said. 'The ransom demand will be telephoned here this time tomorrow. They said there's to be no police action.'

There was a brief pause, then Grandi said, 'Do nothing until I come. I will arrive in eight hours,' and he hung up.

'Kidnapped?' Marvin staggered to his feet, reeled, then sat down again.

'You've been drugged,' Frost said, and going out into the lobby, he picked up the big coffee pot and a cup off the waiting breakfast trays and returned to the guard-room.

Marvin drank the coffee, set down the cup, ran his hand over his face and stared at Frost.

'The girl's been kidnapped?'

'Yep. The snatchers have just telephoned. I've stopped the staff arriving and I've told the guard to let no one out. I've just talked to Grandi. He says we do nothing until he arrives in eight hours. I'm going to take a look around. I want to see if they took one of the boats.'

'Kidnapped? But how?' Marvin shook his head, shut his eyes, opened them and got unsteadily to his feet. 'When?'

'Amando was drugged too. I'll be back,' and Frost left the guardroom. He walked fast down to the harbour. The gate to the harbour stood open. He wondered what Gina was doing right now: probably giggling herself silly with excitement.

Leaving the gate as it was, he walked around the estate. By the time he returned to the villa, it was 09.15.

He found Marvin with Amando in the guardroom. He was glad to see Amando looked utterly stricken. He was white and shaking. Frost was sure that when Grandi arrived, Amando would be skinned.

'She's gone,' he said. 'The boats are all there. Mr Grandi will be here by 16.00.' He sat down, waving the other two to chairs. 'I'm in charge, and it's my neck that'll be chopped.' He talked in his hard cop voice. 'You two were drugged. How could you have been drugged?' He glared at Amando.

'I – I don't know.'

'Then you'd better start thinking!' Frost snapped. 'Did you have a drink last night?'

'I have a glass of milk every night. Suka brings it to me.'

Frost looked at Marvin.

'We had beer, but I opened the cans. That soup! Did it taste odd?'

Marvin had now recovered. He was staring thoughtfully at Frost.

'It tasted fine.'

'It could have been doped, couldn't it?'

'Then why wasn't your soup doped?'

Watch it, Frost warned himself, this sonofabitch is a trained cop.

'This is the way I see it,' he said. 'As I told Mr Grandi, to get at his daughter, there had to be an inside man to neutralise the fence. There are four men on the estate: Mr Amando, you, myself and Suka. You two were drugged because you were both in the villa. I wasn't drugged because I was in my cabin, and there is no way I can reach the guardroom to neutralise the fence without getting attacked by the dogs? Right?'

Marvin's eyes narrowed.

'I guess that's right. Suka, huh?'

'Couldn't be anyone else.' Frost looked at Amando. 'You with me?'

'Yes . . . yes,' he said in a quavering voice. 'I've never trusted Suka.' He got unsteadily to his feet. 'I am feeling bad. I must rest before Mr Grandi comes. I will be in my room,' and he walked unsteadily from the guardroom.

'This is the end of the road for him,' Frost said, as the door closed.

'Let's get that yellow sonofabitch in here and grill him!' Marvin said.

'No! We do nothing until Grandi arrives. Those were his orders. As soon as he arrives, we'll take Suka apart.'

'So we sit around here for eight goddamn hours, doing nothing?'

'That's what I've got to do, but you're officially off-duty. Go and get some sleep.'

Marvin poured more coffee.

'I couldn't sleep.' He drank, then sighed. 'Gee! My kid's going to be disappointed. I promised to take him to the fun fair. I'd better call Mrs Washington and tell her I won't be coming.'

'Why do that? Why disappoint the kid? Grandi won't be here until 16.00. That gives you at least six hours to be with your kid. Go on, see him, and get back here before 14.00. Why not?'

Marvin hesitated, then his face lit up.

'I've never broken a promise to him . . . not ever. Do you think it'll be all right, Mike?'

'Sure. I'll just have to sit around, counting my fingers. The action won't start until Grandi gets here. Go on, get off.'

Still Marvin hesitated.

'How about Suka?'

'We have him trapped,' Frost said. 'The guard won't let him out and the fence is electrified. I intend to stay right here by the telephone in case they call again. I intend to lock myself in when you've gone. No problem.'

'Well, then if you're sure, I'll get off.'

'I'll alert the guard to let you out. Have a ball with your kid.' Frost reached for the telephone and gave the guard instructions to let Marvin out and let him in on his return, then he went on to the guard, 'Mr Grandi will be arriving around 16.00. Let him in,' and he hung up.

After some twenty minutes, he saw Marvin drive away in the T.R.7.

At their last meeting, Frost had told Silk of his idea of making Suka the fall guy, and Silk had approved. He had told Silk what he then was going to do, and again Silk approved.

'One Jap less is one Jap less,' Frost had said.

He got to his feet and went to the door leading to the villa and raising his voice, he called, 'Suka! Hey, Suka!'

Leaving the door open, he returned to the desk and sat down.

After a delay, Suka appeared in the doorway.

'I want you to go down to the harbour right away,' Frost said. 'When I checked the grounds, I found the harbour gate open. I forgot to shut it. I have to stay here by the telephone. Will you go down and shut it?'

Suka nodded.

Frost got up and pressed the button that neutralised the fence.

'The current's off,' he said, trying to speak casually. 'Go ahead.'

Suka nodded and hurried away.

Frost was aware his heart was thumping. He had never killed a man, but what was one Jap less?

Drawing in a deep breath, he pressed the red button, turning on the current. The moment Suka touched the gate, he would be dead.

Seven

At exactly 14.00, Jack Marvin walked into the guardroom.

'Hi, Mike! Any excitements?'

It had been a long wait, and Frost was jittery. Suka hadn't returned, that must mean he was dead.

It was the only way, Frost had argued to himself. Having made Suka the fall guy, it would be too dangerous for him to live. From time to time, he wanted to go down to the harbour, but if Amando came to the guardroom and found him missing it would poke a hole in the story he was going to tell.

He was going to tell Grandi that he had immediately suspected Suka, and had taken precautions to make sure Suka couldn't leave the estate. He had told the guards to let no one out and he had electrified the fence. Obviously, he would say, Suka got in a panic and had decided to take off in one of the boats, forgetting the fence was electrified and had been killed. The police would have to be called, but Frost felt he could deal with them. Suka had been killed accidentally.

Marvin was the man to find the body.

'Not a thing,' Frost said, 'but I'm goddamn hungry. You eaten?'

Marvin grinned.

'I've been eating hotdogs and ice cream with the kid for the past hour. Why didn't you tell Suka to get you something?'

'I thought I'd wait until you got back. Be a pal, and tell him to hustle up a snack.'

'Sure.'

It was over ten minutes before Marvin hurried into the guardroom. He looked worried.

'No sign of him. I've checked his cabin.' He stared at Frost. 'You don't think he's scrammed?'

'No way,' Frost said impatiently. 'He's around the estate some place. Take a look, Jack. I've got to stay by the telephone. Watch it! The current's on. Don't touch the fence.'

'Okay,' and Marvin hurried away.

Frost went to the refrigerator and took out a can of beer. He drank the beer slowly. In a few minutes, Marvin would find Suka's body. He finished the beer, lit a cigarette, then walked to the guardroom door and looked along the path leading to the harbour. Minutes ticked by, then he saw Marvin come running up the path. The alarm on Marvin's face sent Frost's heart thumping. So Suka was dead! Frost felt a chill run down his spine. He had murdered a man!

Marvin was shouting something as he ran, but Frost didn't register what he was saying.

'What the hell's up?' he exclaimed, and went to meet Marvin.

'He's scrammed!' Marvin blurted out, coming to a halt. 'The harbour gate's open, and the motorboat's gone!'

Frost felt as if an ironclad fist had hit him below the heart. He stood motionless, chills running over him as he stared at Marvin.

'Hear me!' Marvin snapped. 'He's scrammed!'

Frost made an effort and pulled himself together.

'Can't be!'

'The gate's open, and the motorboat's gone!' Marvin said.

To gain time to think, Frost shoved by him and ran down to the harbour.

His mind worked like lightning as he ran. Had Suka overheard him telling Amando and Marvin that he (Suka) was the inside man, then seeing the open gate, had bolted?

There could be no other explanation. The fact was he had escaped! Frost felt a sudden relief. He hadn't committed murder! But Suka at liberty could be dangerous. He must alert Silk.

He reached the harbour and saw how easily anyone could slip down to the boats without touching the open door nor the fence.

He was still standing there, his mind active when Marvin joined him.

'I've turned off the current,' Marvin said and closed the gate. 'How the hell did he open the gate without being electrocuted?'

'My guess he must have listened to us talking,' Frost said. 'Like a dope, I didn't turn on the current until you left the guardroom to change. In those few minutes, he must have scrammed. I never thought of checking on him once you had gone. I locked myself in and stayed put.'

Marvin stared at him, his expression worried.

'Grandi will love you, Mike. You should have turned on the current when we were talking.'

'And he'll love you too,' Frost snapped. 'You should have been here instead of at the funfair with your kid.'

'Aw, come on, Mike. You're in charge. You told me to go.'

'Okay, okay. Anyway what the hell does it matter? We're both going to lose our jobs.'

'I guess. Look, Mike, I have friends at the cop house. How's about me asking Lepski to pick up Suka? I can say some valuables are missing and ...'

'No way,' Frost said curtly. 'We do nothing until Grandi arrives. Anyway, we now know for sure Suka was the inside man. I'm going to get myself something to eat. Suppose you walk around, check his cabin, see if he's taken his clothes.'

'Yeah.'

Leaving Marvin, Frost hurried back to the guardroom. He locked the door leading to the villa, then snatched up the telephone receiver. He dialled the number of the Ace of Spades.

Umney came on the line.

'Suka got away in a motorboat,' Frost said, speaking fast. 'The boat has a big G on the stern. Find and fix him.'

'Will do,' Umney said, and hung up.

Frost then went up to Amando's room, opened the door and walked in. He found Amando lying on the bed, his face ashen. Amando opened his eyes and stared glassily at Frost.

'I am very ill,' he mumbled. 'My heart . . . get a doctor.'

Frost stared down at him. Faking? He thought not, but he couldn't care less about Amando.

'You'll need more than a doctor when Grandi arrives,' he said, and left the room.

He found some cold cuts in the kitchen refrigerator and made himself a couple of sandwiches, then he returned to the guardroom.

As he was eating the second sandwich, Marvin came in.

'Old Creepy's sick,' Frost said. 'He's had a heart attack.'

'To hell with him,' Marvin said. 'Look what I've found in Suka's cabin.' He put a small box on the desk. 'A sophisticated bug.'

Frost opened the box and stared at the black button. This was a limpet bug that was powerful enough to record a conversation from a considerable distance. He looked at the empty socket by the bug that told him there had been a second bug.

'That's how he heard us talking,' Marvin said. 'I bet the other bug is somewhere right here.'

Frost snatched up the telephone and up-ended it. The second bug was attached to the base of the telephone. He whirled around on Marvin.

'Was there a recorder in his cabin?'

'Yeah, but no cassette. I checked.'

Frost removed the bug and put it in the box. He realised the danger of this discovery immediately.

'More evidence for Grandi,' he said, forcing his voice to sound casual.

'Hey, Mike!' Marvin was pointing to the gun rack. 'There's a .38 missing!'

Frost looked at the gun rack. There should have been four .38 police specials on hooks on the rack: there were only three.

'How the hell did he take that?'

'When you were checking the grounds and when I went up to Amando,' Marvin said. 'We both should have seen it was missing.'

'Okay, okay,' Frost said. 'We needn't spell it all out to Grandi. Suppose you go up and take another look at Amando. If he is really bad, call an ambulance and let's get him to hospital before Grandi arrives. Fix it, will you?'

Leaving Marvin, he went fast to his cabin. He examined his telephone, made sure it wasn't bugged, then called the Ace of Spades. This time he got Silk.

Quickly, he explained the situation, then went on, 'If Suka left the tape running, he has evidence I fingered him as the inside man, and more dangerous, I told him the gate was open and to shut it. If he gets to Grandi, my cover's blown. He'll be at the airport waiting for Grandi to arrive. You've got to fix him before Grandi arrives. Watch it! He's armed!'

'I'll have the airport covered in ten minutes,' Silk said. 'When is Grandi arriving?'

'Around 15.00. New York arrival.'

'Keep your cool, Mike,' Silk said quietly. 'It's going along well. Don't forget we have Grandi over a barrel.'

'Yeah, but I want to keep my cover. How's the girl?'

'No problem. I gave her a reefer, and she is way out,' and Silk hung up.

Frost wiped his sweating hands on his slacks, then returned to the guardroom where he found Marvin on the telephone, ordering an ambulance.

'He looks as if he's going to croak,' Marvin said as he hung up.

'One headache less.' Frost picked up the telephone receiver and alerted the guard at the entrance to let the ambulance in.

'Hell!' the guard exploded. 'You sure sound as if you have real trouble up there.'

'Tell that to Mr Grandi when he arrives. He'll love the sound of your voice,' Frost snarled, and hung up.

* * *

The ambulance taking Amando to the Paradise Clinic, hadn't been gone more than ten minutes, when Frost heard the sound of an approaching helicopter. The machine hovered over the estate, then gently settled down on the big lawn.

'Here he is,' Frost said, as both he and Marvin moved fast out of the guardroom. 'Action stations!'

As Grandi climbed from the machine, Frost hurried across the lawn to meet him.

Grandi paused to say something to the pilot, then came striding forward, his face a stone mask, his eyes glittering dangerously.

'Where's Amando?' he barked as Frost paused before him.

'He's had a heart attack, sir. The ambulance has just taken him to the Paradise Clinic.'

Grandi stared at Frost.

'Then he's lucky,' he snarled. 'Come to my study in ten minutes,' and moving by Frost, ignoring Marvin, he strode into the villa.

'Stick around, Jack,' Frost said, and breaking into a run, he went to his cabin, shut himself in and grabbing the telephone, dialled the Ace of Spades.

Silk came on the line.

'Did you get Suka?' Frost asked, speaking low and fast.

'No sign of the sonofabitch,' Silk said. 'No sign of Grandi either.'

'He's here. He must have flown to Miami and taken a chopper. He arrived a minute ago.'

'Then Suka couldn't have contacted him. We'll keep hunting.'

'Find him and fix him,' Frost said and hung up.

Bracing himself, he walked to the villa, entered, then stood in the big hall, waiting.

Five minutes later, Grandi jerked open the door of his study.

'Okay, Frost, let's have it,' he said, and walked to his desk and sat down.

Although his heart was thumping, Frost played it cool. He pulled up a chair and sat down, facing Grandi.

'I told you, sir, that the only way your daughter could be kidnapped was for an inside man to organise the kidnapping. The inside man is the Jap . . . Suka. The evidence all points to him.' Frost went on to explain that Amando's and Marvin's drinks were doped, how he, himself, was a prisoner in his cabin because of the dogs, and how Marvin had found Suka gone and one of the boats missing.

'Okay,' Grandi said abruptly. 'I accept that. Then what happened?'

'My guess is Suka was well paid. He neutralised the fence and the kidnappers came in, grabbed Miss Grandi and took her away in their own boat. At 07.45, I left my cabin, found Marvin drugged, called Suka who found Amando drugged. I then checked the grounds and found the harbour gate open. I immediately suspected Suka, and I told Amando and Marvin my suspicions. Suka had a bug in here.' Frost paused to produce the box containing the two bugs. He put the box on the desk. 'He overheard my talk with Amando and Marvin, panicked and bolted. It wasn't until after talking with Amando and Marvin that I electrified the fence again and warned the guard at the entrance to let no one out. If there is a fault, sir, I should have immediately electrified the fence, but I missed out on the guardroom being bugged.'

Grandi looked up and glared at Frost.

'We'll go into who missed out and who didn't later,' he said. 'My daughter has been kidnapped. What's the next move?'

'Two moves,' Frost said, beginning to relax. He was thinking if only Silk could find and fix Suka, the big problem looked solved. At least, Grandi was accepting Suka as the inside man. 'This is up to you. Number one would be to alert the police that Miss Grandi has been kidnapped. The kidnapper warned against this, but it could be done providing the police don't move into action.'

Grandi made an impatient movement.

'No police. What's the second move?'

'We wait for a ransom demand, sir. The kidnapper said he would telephone tomorrow at 08.00. Now, if we alerted the police they could tap our telephone and get a fix on where he is phoning from, but it will probably be from a call box, and it could be dangerous.'

Grandi nodded.

'We wait for the ransom demand,' he said. 'No police.'

'Yes, sir.' A pause, then, Frost went on, 'I've told the staff to take the day off, but they'll be in tomorrow as usual. If there is anything I or Marvin can do for you, sir, you just have to say.'

'I will stay at the Spanish Bay hotel,' Grandi said. 'Tomorrow at seven o'clock, I will be here. I want you to take the ransom call, and I want you to handle it, Frost.' He got to his feet, then stared thoughtfully at Frost. 'Do you think I'll get her back?'

'Yes, sir, so long as you go along with the kidnappers. From my experience, once the ransom is paid, they deliver.'

'I am relying on your experience,' Grandi said, then he walked out and leaving the villa, he crossed the lawn, got in the helicopter and was whisked away.

Frost grabbed the telephone and again dialled the Ace of Spades.

'It's going well this end,' he said as Silk came on the

line. 'Grandi is staying at the Spanish Bay. Stake it out in case Suka arrives.'

'I told you, didn't I?' Silk said. 'We have this fink over a barrel. Don't worry about the Jap. I'll fix him.'

Frost replaced the telephone receiver. He felt in need of a drink. Grandi had been easy to handle. He drew in a deep breath. So long as Silk could find and fix Suka there would be no problem. He looked at his watch. The time was 16.15. He walked over to the big cocktail cabinet and poured himself a stiff whisky. He felt he deserved it. He drank the whisky at one swallow, then leaving the room, he went to the guardroom where Marvin was pacing up and down.

'How did it go?' Marvin asked.

'No problem so far,' Frost said. 'Tomorrow is the day when the ransom demand arrives. He is surprisingly under control. I thought I was in for a hell of a time, but I guess he just wants his daughter back.'

Marvin relaxed.

'Who would want a little bitch like that back?'

'That's his choice. Look, Jack, there'll be no action now until tomorrow morning. I'm going to find myself a dolly bird. I feel in need of some relaxation. You can do what you like: either stay around here or go to see your son again.'

Marvin looked worried.

'The kidnapper might telephone again.'

'Aw, skip it, Jack! You be here at six o'clock tomorrow. Nothing's going to happen. I'm going to get changed.'

Marvin suddenly grinned.

'You're the boss. I guess I'll get changed too.'

'You take the T.R. I'll take the Lamborghini. I fancy driving that heap.'

Forty minutes later, Frost drove into an empty parking place outside the Ace of Spades. At this hour, the restaurant and bar were deserted. He found Silk and Goble playing gin in the room above the swimming pool. As soon as Frost entered, the two men threw down their cards, and Silk said, 'What are you doing here, Mike?'

'There's no action until you put in the ransom note,' Frost said, sitting down at the table. 'How's Gina?'

'She's fine. Right now Ross is keeping her company.' Silk smiled his evil smile. 'They're probably screwing.'

'She's an enthusiast. How about Suka?'

Silk shrugged.

'I don't know. He's vanished. My guess is he was scared shitless and has taken off. I've got the Spanish Bay staked out and Marcia is around there. Forget Suka. We don't have to bother about that fink.'

But Frost felt uneasy.

'If he got to Grandi with that tape, I could be in a lot of trouble.'

'How did Grandi react?'

'He surprised me. I thought he was certain to blow his cork, but all he seems interested in is getting the girl back. He told me he wanted me to handle the deal.'

Silk nodded.

'That's fine. Then when I telephone tomorrow I'll say someone is to come to the Three Square motel to get the ransom note . . . that'll be you.' He regarded Frost. 'Grandi's tricky. How about the cops?'

'I suggested he should tell the cops, but he killed that idea. No cops.'

'Going our way,' Silk said.

'Yeah.' Frost got to his feet. 'I'll have a word with Gina. She's in Marcia's room?'

'That's it,' Goble said, picking up his cards. 'Knock twice before you enter.' He grinned. 'Ross has been with her for the past three hours, but they still could be active.'

Frost made his way along the corridor to Marcia's room, paused outside the door, listened, heard nothing, then rapped. He waited, rapped again, waited, then frowning, a sudden uneasiness creeping over him, he eased open the door and stepped into the room.

Umney, naked, lay sprawled across the big bed, blood seeping from a wound in his head.

Frost looked around the room, then, moving fast, looked into the bathroom. Except for himself and Umney who was moving out of unconsciousness, the room was empty.

No Gina.

* * *

Frost, Silk and Goble crowded around Umney as he sat on the edge of the bed, holding his head.

'We were doing a saddle job,' Umney said thickly, 'then from out of nowhere she produced a gun and gun butted me. I hadn't a chance.'

A gun!

So it had been Gina who had taken the .38 from the armoury rack, and not Suka, Frost thought.

'She's gone, you goddamn creep!' Silk snarled.

Umney moaned.

'Hear me!' Silk banged his fist on Umney's shoulder. 'When was this?'

'We got going as soon as I arrived . . . around two o'clock.'

'Three hours! She could be anywhere!' Silk swung around to Goble. 'Check the cars!'

Goble left the room at a run.

Frost stood back and he watched Silk who began to move around the room. He paused and stared at Frost.

'You told me she wanted to be snatched!' he said. 'You didn't say . . .'

'Aw, shut up!' Frost barked. 'How did she get out of here without being seen?'

'There's an exit at the end of the corridor that leads to the car park. That's the way she went.'

Frost went to the big range of closets. He opened doors, slammed them shut, then turned to Silk.

'She's taken her suitcase.'

142

Goble rushed in.

'My car's missing!'

Umney got unsteadily to his feet and went into the bathroom.

'Where would she go?' Silk demanded, glaring at Frost.

'How the hell do I know, but I do know she wouldn't go back to Orchid Villa. She's taken off to do her thing.'

Silk turned to Goble.

'Send the word out, Mitch. Get all our contacts working on this.'

When Goble had gone, Silk went on to Frost, 'You're sure she won't go back to the Grandi's place?'

'Sure. That's why she wanted to be kidnapped.'

'Then the operation is still on,' Silk said. 'Grandi won't know she's scrammed. So long as she keeps away from him, he'll think we have her.'

Frost thought about it, then nodded.

'Yeah. Then we go ahead on schedule?'

Umney came out of the bathroom and began to dress. He kept moaning to himself, but neither Silk nor Frost paid any attention to him.

'What's the chance of finding her?' Frost asked.

'I have contacts. Mitch will have alerted them. If she's still around, we'll find her.'

'Now, wait a moment. Do we want to find her? Isn't it better to let her lose herself?'

Silk thought, then grinned.

'Yeah, but we should know if she's around here. If she's taken off to Miami or some place we have no problem.'

'If we don't deliver her back to Grandi, he'll turn on the heat,' Frost said uneasily.

'How can he, unless he wants to go to jail for fifteen years? We'll play it as we wrote it. It'll stand up.'

Umney said, 'She's crazy in the head and she's got a gun.'

'Who the hell cares?' Silk snarled. 'So long as she keeps out of sight.'

But Frost's police trained mind saw trouble ahead.

'She's unpredictable. Umney's right. There's something about her . . . she know's the three of us. If Grandi catches up with her, she could talk.'

'So Grandi doesn't catch up with her,' Silk said. 'We go ahead. It'll work out.'

'Let's get this thing on the rails,' Frost said. 'Why wait until tomorrow? Give me the ransom demand now. The longer we wait, the chances of Gina being picked up either by your people or Grandi makes for trouble.' He thought for a moment, then went on. 'I'll tell Grandi I wanted a change of scene while waiting for the ransom note to be delivered tomorrow morning. I took a car and drove down to the beach. After a swim, I found the ransom demand in the car. What do you think?'

Goble came in.

'The word's gone out. If the car's around here, it'll be found.'

'Mike wants to hurry this up,' Silk said. 'He's got something.' Looking at Frost, he went on, 'Tell him.'

Frost repeated what he had said to Silk. After thought, Goble nodded.

'Yeah. Why not? The longer we wait, the bigger the risk.'

Twenty minutes later, Frost was driving to the Spanish Bay hotel with the ransom demand. The time was now 18.15. He pulled up outside the hotel. Seeing the Lamborghini, the top-hatted negro hurried down the steps and opened the door of the car.

'Park it,' Frost said, and entering the hotel lobby, he crossed to the reception desk. 'Mr Grandi,' he said to the suave clerk who regarded him with slightly raised eyebrows.

'Your name, sir?'

'Mike Frost.'

The reception clerk went into an inner office. There was a delay, then he came out and nodded to Frost.

'Suite 67, Mr Frost. Take the elevator to the eighth floor and turn left as you leave. Suite 67 will be facing you.'

As Frost rode up in the elevator, he wondered how Grandi would react to the ransom demand. He was distinctly uneasy, but he reminded himself that, with luck, in a month's time, he would be worth five million dollars.

The elevator doors swished open and he moved into a heavily carpeted, broad corridor. A door with silver numerals '67' faced him. Crossing the corridor, he rapped on the door and waited.

There was a moment's delay, then the door jerked open and Grandi regarded him.

'What do you want?' Grandi barked. 'Something happened?'

'Yes, sir. I think I have the ransom note.'

Grandi's eyes narrowed. He stepped back, motioning Frost in, then he walked across the large living-room and sat down behind a paper-strewn desk. He waved Frost to a chair.

'Tell me.'

'As nothing was to happen until tomorrow morning, sir,' Frost said, 'I went down to the beach. I spent an hour down there. On returning to the car, I found this envelope, addressed to you, on the driving seat.'

He leaned forward and dropped the envelope Silk had given him on the desk.

Grandi stared at it, then at Frost.

'Go down to the bar and wait,' Grandi said. 'I will call you when I want you.'

'Yes, sir.'

Frost got to his feet and walked to the door. As he was leaving the suite, Grandi picked up the envelope. He was slitting open the envelope with a paper knife as Frost closed the door.

In the bar, Frost ordered a whisky on the rocks and sat at an isolated table. There were only a few people in the bar, and no one did more than give him a cursory glance.

He waited, and while he waited, he thought of Gina, wondering where she was. He was sure she would keep herself hidden. So what did it matter where she was?

Grandi would sign the document transferring thirty million dollars to Silk's Swiss account, then the four of them would take off together, and Grandi could whistle for Gina.

He was still thinking of what he would do once he got his hands on all that money when the barman came over to him.

'Mr Grandi is asking for you, sir.'

Frost got to his feet, squared his shoulders and walked to the elevator. This was it! he told himself. It was unlikely Grandi would tell him about the ransom demand, but he would indicate that he was paying, and that was all Frost wanted to know.

He rapped on the door of suite 67 and heard Grandi call, 'Come on in.'

He found Grandi at his desk, a big cigar between his fat fingers, his face a hard expressionless mask.

'We have some talking to do, Frost,' Grandi said. 'Sit down.'

'Yes, sir.'

Uneasy, Frost sat in the chair opposite Grandi's desk.

Grandi opened a drawer in his desk and took from it a tape cassette. He held it up so Frost could see it.

'Do you know what this is, Frost?'

Frost felt his heart give a lurch. So Suka had somehow got to Grandi. Keeping his face expressionless, reminding himself that there was nothing Grandi could do unless he opted to go to jail for tax fraud, he said, 'Yes, sir. I know what it is.'

'Suka met me at the Miami airport,' Grandi said and smiled. He looked like a vicious hungry wolf. 'How much did they pay you, Frost, to be the inside man?'

'Don't let's waste time, Grandi,' Frost said in his cop voice. 'Sign that transfer and give it to me. That's all you have to do unless you don't want your daughter back and you fancy a fifteen year stretch in an Italian jail.'

Grandi picked up the document which was lying on his desk and studied it.

'Not even a good try,' he said. 'I don't imagine you worked out this kidnapping yourself. I am not interested in your associates. I intend to deal with you. With the ransom demand, as you know, are specimens of transfers to a Swiss bank. These are illegal transfers as the currency regulations in Italy forbid money leaving the country, but what your associates haven't appreciated is the fact that transfer of money from Italy is illegal only to the vast majority.' Grandi regarded Frost. 'I am not the vast majority. To have obtained these photocopies, your associates must have corrupted my chief accountant, Guiseppe Vessi, who handled the transfers. You may have wondered why you have been kept waiting for an hour before I talk with you. Let me tell you: I was arranging that Vessi ceases to exist. No one ever betrays me and remains alive!'

Frost, staring at the ruthless, vicious face, knew Grandi wasn't bluffing.

'Even with Vessi out of the way,' he said, 'that still doesn't keep you out of jail.'

'Little man!' Grandi laughed. 'There is only one man in Italy who could make trouble for me, and he is my close friend: the Minister of Finance. Suppose your associates are stupid enough to send copies of these Swiss transactions to the tax authorities. They would pass them to the Minister of Finance who would sweep them under the carpet. He is as much involved as I am. In fact, little man, I will tell you for the past three years I have allowed him to syphon off some of his money to my account. Your associates are so ill-informed of the Italian scene that they don't realise that any deal can be arranged in Italy as long as you have enough power.' He leaned forward, stabbing his finger at Frost. 'And I have all the power in the world!'

'If you want your daughter back, you'll sign that document!' Frost snapped. 'I'm not interested in your machinations. Just sign it!'

Grandi studied him, then drew the document to him and signed with a flourish.

'If that's all you want. When do I get my daughter back?'

'As soon as the money has been transferred to Zurich,' Frost said. This was a moment of triumph. He snatched up the document.

Grandi shook his head.

'That won't do. She will be dead of old age by then.'

With a feeling that he was being tricked, Frost glared at Grandi.

'What the hell do you mean?'

'Your associates didn't do their homework,' Grandi said. 'The Lugano numbered account belongs to myself and three friends, and one of them is the Minister of Finance who I have just mentioned. None of us can draw out money without the the other three adding their signatures. I can tell you their names, but I can assure you they wouldn't sign.' He lifted his heavy shoulders in an Italian shrug. 'Unfortunately, they have no interest in my daughter.'

Frost flung the document back on the desk.

'If you want Gina back alive, you'd better persuade your friends to sign!'

'That would be a waste of time to try. They certainly don't value my daughter at twenty million dollars.' Grandi leaned forward and gave his wolf smile. 'Let us approach this business from another angle.'

'How much will you pay to get your daughter back?' Frost demanded, aware now his hands had turned moist.

'Ah! That is a good question.' Grandi drew on his cigar and released a rich-smelling smoke. 'So we are agreed the ransom isn't to be twenty million dollars?'

Frost hesitated.

'This is something I must discuss with my associates, he said. 'Give me a proposal, and then we will consider it.'

'Now you are growing up, little man,' Grandi said. 'Here is my proposal. You will return Gina here within four hours. In return, I will take no legal proceedings against you or your associates. That is my proposal.'

'How much money?' Frost demanded.

Grandi shook his head.

'No money. Send her back unharmed, and I'll forget you and your stupid associates exist.'

Frost forced a laugh. Even to him it sounded hollow.

'No way. We're in this for money. Suppose we say five million? She's worth five million to you. How about it?'

'No money, and I will tell you why.' He opened a drawer in his desk and took out two reels of tape. 'Take these. I have the originals, but I want you to have them so that you and your stupid associates can understand how badly you have planned this operation.' Grandi pulled on his cigar, then went on, 'When I rented Orchid Villa, I took precautions. Now I will tell you about Suka. He was a security and an electronic expert working for the Tokyo police. I bought him. I gave him the problem of making the villa safe. Apart from all the security gimmicks, he also installed a telephone tap with a continuous tape recording. Every call in and out of the villa has been recorded. The copies of these tapes which I am giving you tell a story. I know about Marcia Goolden, a whore, who lives at this hotel. I know you have been in contact with her and Amando visits her. Obviously, she drugged Amando when he was with her as you drugged Marvin. I know you told your associates to murder Suka. A voice print will identify you, and if I give the tapes to the police, they will have no problem indicting you. I know too you have been screwing my daughter. Her room has always been bugged. My daughter is mentally sick, but she is still my daughter and I'm going to have her back! Return her to me in four hours and I won't take proceedings.' Grandi stubbed out his cigar. 'Take the tapes, talk to your associates, but remember . . . if she isn't here by ten o'clock tonight, you will spend twenty years in jail.'

Frost tried to say something but the words wouldn't come. He got unsteadily to his feet.

'One more thing, little man,' Grandi said. 'It might occur to you that the way out for you would be to kill me.'

He smiled wolfishly. 'Don't try it. I am very well protected.' He leaned forward, his face a snarling mask of rage, and he screamed at Frost, 'Get out of my sight!'

* * *

The four men sat around the table, a tape player before them and they listened to Frost saying:

'*Did you get Suka?*'

Silk's voice.

'*No sign of the sonofabitch. No sign of Grandi either.*'

Frost snapped off the player.

'We've got to find her and return her, Silk!'

Silk rubbed the side of his jaw, thought for a moment, then shrugged.

'It looked good.' He stared with his one glittering eye at Umney who looked pale and he kept his hand to his aching head. 'You sure fell down on this one, Ross. You should have dug deeper.'

'You shouldn't have touched it at all,' Umney snarled. 'We told you no way, but you wouldn't listen!'

'Wrap up!' Frost exclaimed. 'How do we find her?'

'She left my car at the waterfront,' Goble said. 'I've got men down there.' He got up, went to the telephone and put a call through. He talked quietly for two or three minutes, then hung up.

The others looked at him expectantly.

'She hasn't taken a boat,' he said. 'There are around fifteen small hotels down there. She's probably holed up in one of them, waiting until it gets dark.'

'Or she left the car there as a stall and walked to the bus stop and is in Miami by now,' Silk said

Frost got to his feet.

'We have less than three hours to find her! You get down to the waterfront,' he was speaking to Goble. 'You,' turning to Silk, 'cover the bus station. You've got her description. I'm going back to the villa to search her room. I might come up with something.' He paused at

150

the door. To Umney he said, 'Stay by the telephone. I'll be calling in for progress reports,' then he left the room at a run.

Driving just within the speed limit, he arrived back at the villa as the car's dashboard clock showed 19.20. Aware time was rapidly running out, he dashed up the stairs and into Gina's room. He feverishly searched through every drawer and cupboard, went through the contents of the little desk by the window, but came up with nothing. By now the time was 20.00. Two hours more to find her!

He snatched up the telephone receiver and called Umney.

'Any news?'

'Lu's just checked out the bus station. No one's seen her, and we have good contacts there. Our best bet is the waterfront. Lu's on his way down there.'

An idea dropped into Frost's mind. He remembered what Gina had said to him: *I don't give a shit about money. I just want to take off and do my thing.*

'Is there a way out, hippy colony around here?'

'Where isn't there? Sure, the freaks get together at Paddler's Creek. Do you think she could be there?'

'I don't know. Where's this place?'

'Around ten miles out of the city towards Key West,' Umney told him. 'They have these swing festivals there.'

'Where do I find it?'

'Go along the highway south. There's a motel on the right hand side. Twin Oakes. Take the first turning past the motel on your right and that takes you down to the beach. You think she's there?'

'How the hell do I know, but I'm going to look,' and Frost hung up.

He got into the Lamborghini and sat for a long moment, thinking, then he drove fast to the Spanish Bay hotel.

Five minutes later he was once again facing Grandi.

Frost now was all cop. He sat down, his face as hard and as expressionless as Grandi's.

'You have her?' Grandi snapped.

'No. I'm going to level with you,' Frost said. 'She wanted to be kidnapped. Okay, I helped her, but it was she who neutralised the fence. She went to the harbour with a suitcase where my associates picked her up. They took her to the Ace of Spades.'

'I know all that,' Grandi snarled. 'It's on tape!'

'But what you don't know, she got one of my associates into bed and while they were copulating she bashed him with a gun and took off. We're trying to find her. Now listen carefully, Grandi, she wants you dead, and she has a gun. I don't want any more of this crap about finding her in four hours. We'll find her, but it will take more than four hours. This is up to you.'

'So she's got away?' Grandi seemed to shrink a little.

'That's it. She took a car. We found it on the waterfront. We've checked. She hasn't tried to hire a boat. We are checking the hotels.' Frost paused, then went on, 'How sick is she?'

Grandi clenched his fists.

'So sick she should have been committed,' he said as if the words were being dragged from him, 'but I couldn't do that to her. Instead, I put her behind an electrified fence. Amando is a mental specialist in charge of her. His weekly reports show she is deteriorating. In Rome, she took a massive dose of L.S.D. It shocked her brain out of balance. Amando describes her as a sexual lunatic. That's how sick she is . . . but I don't give a damn what she has become. She is my daughter, and I want her back!' He glared at Frost. 'It was through you, she escaped, so bring her back or I'll fix you as I have fixed Vessi! Make no mistake about that!'

'She hates you, Grandi. She wants you dead. She has a gun. She told me you want to screw her,' Frost said.

'I've listened to all her sick talk on the tape,' Grandi said. 'She didn't know what she was saying. Even if I dropped dead tomorrow, she wouldn't be able to touch a dollar. It is all in trust.' He paused, then pointed his finger at Frost, 'Find her, and bring her to me. Do that, and I will pay you five million dollars.'

Frost became alert. He leaned forward.

'You mean that? How will you pay me?'

Grandi shrugged.

'As you like. Any bank anywhere . . . cash. I want her back!'

'Are you really making a deal with me or are you just conning me?' Frost said.

'It's a deal. I am too big a man to go back on my word. Bring her to me, and I will give you my word I will pay you five million dollars, but if you don't find her, I again give you my word: consider yourself dead!'

Frost got to his feet.

'I'll find her. It could take time, but for five million, I will find her!'

Leaving the hotel, he stood for a long time by the Lamborghini. Around him was the murmur of voices. A swing band played on the hotel terrace. The big, yellow moon floated in a cloudless sky. The time was 21.05.

Five million dollars!

I am too big a man to go back on my word.

Frost accepted that.

The wheel had turned full circle. Now he had to find her.

* * *

Frost left the Lamborghini under a clump of mango trees, and walked the rest of the way.

He could hear the sound of guitars and singing voices, and as he drew nearer, he picked up the smell of unwashed bodies and reefer smoke, so he knew he was approaching the hippy colony.

There was plenty of cover and he moved cautiously. He could now see camp fires burning and figures moving around. He paused behind a sea shrub and watched.

There were some hundred or so young people milling

153

around, talking, singing, some dancing by themselves: aimless, shiftless movements, and he guessed they were high.

Somehow, he told himself, Gina just might be there. This scene would be what she called her thing, but how to find her?

He moved to another clump of shrubs which brought him nearer to the camp fires. He waited, searching, watching, but he couldn't see any girl milling around who resembled Gina.

Should he walk into that mob and start asking questions? He decided it wouldn't be safe. They all seemed pretty high, and he didn't fancy the idea of walking into the midst of them.

He squatted down on his haunches. Maybe, if he waited long enough . . .

He watched and waited for longer than an hour, but still he saw no sign of Gina. Then just when he was deciding to give up, he heard a faint rustle behind him. A snake? He remained motionless, his muscles tense, ready to spring aside, but waiting.

'Stay right where you are, man,' a voice said behind him, 'or you'll lose a kidney.'

He felt the prick of a knife in his back, and he relaxed. Snakes bothered him, but not a man with a knife.

'I'm all still,' he said.

'We don't like peepers around here, man,' the voice said.

Frost judged the speaker was young, but sure of himself.

'Sorry,' Frost made his voice sound humble. 'You kids seem to be having a ball,' then he acted. His right hand swept behind him, smashing against a wrist. He heard a yelp of pain as he spun around. He dropped on the crouching figure, flattening the man into the sand. His hands fastened on the lean, sweating neck.

In the strong moonlight, he saw the Afro hair-do, the black glistening skin.

154

'Going to be good, sonny?' he said, his knee hard into the small of the negro's back.

'Sure . . . sure . . . ' the black gasped. 'You're killing me!'

Frost looked quickly around. He saw the switch blade knife glittering in the moonlight some ten feet away. He was on his feet and had gathered up the knife before the black struggled to a sitting position.

'Jesus, man!' the black gasped. 'I didn't know you were fuzz. Honestly, I thought you were a peeper!'

Frost threw the knife far into the dark shrubs.

He regarded the black. He was lean, young, with big wild eyes and a scraggly chin beard. He was dressed in a chequered shirt and jeans.

'What's your name, sonny?' Frost asked quietly.

'I'm Buck. I swear I wasn't going to hurt you. We don't like peepers around here.'

'I'm not a cop, Buck,' Frost said, and walking slowly up to the black, he dropped in the sand beside him. 'I'm looking for someone.'

'You go right on looking man,' Buck said. 'I'll just scram.'

Frost gripped the lean wrist and wrenched up the shirt sleeve. He didn't have to see the puncture marks, he could feel them. This youth was a vein shooter.

Buck tried to jerk free, but Frost easily held his wrist.

'Want to make a hundred bucks?' Frost said.

Buck became tense.

'You wouldn't be kidding, man?'

'When did you last have a fix?'

Buck mumbled something, and again tried to break Frost's hold.

'Listen, Buck, I want you to look around among your friends. I am looking for a girl with red hair: she's special. If she's here, she can't have been here longer than three hours. She might even have come and gone. If you spot her, don't do anything, just come back here and tell me. If you spot her, you get a hundred bucks. If you don't spot her, you get fifty. Okay?'

'A girl with red hair?'

'That's it. You can't mistake her. It's a special red: not tinted: natural. She's around twenty years of age: good body.'

Buck got to his feet as Frost released his wrist.

'A hundred bucks, man?'

'Yep.' Frost took out his billfold and showed the youth a hundred dollar bill. 'All yours if you spot her.'

'You wait right here, man. Don't you move away.'

'I'll be here, and Buck, if you spot her, just keep going. Just come here and tell me.'

'Okay, man.'

Frost watched the black youth walk quickly and unsteadily towards the camp fires. He watched him moving around. A girl went up to him, but Buck shoved her aside. He finally disappeared into the smoke and the gloom.

Suppose this black youth got some of his friends and tried to jump him, Frost thought. He had shown Buck he had a wallet of money.

Crouching, he moved back until he reached the shelter of a long line of mango trees. He loosened his gun in its holster, then leaning against a tree trunk, sure he was hidden, but could still see the camp fires, he waited.

It was a long wait, then just when he was deciding he wasn't going to see Buck again, and as the hands of his watch moved to 23.15, he saw Buck coming at a jog-trot, and alone.

Buck paused by the shrub and looked wildly around. Frost could see sweat pouring down his black skin, lit by the moonlight.

'Okay, Buck,' he called softly. 'I'm right over here.'

Buck shambled towards him and paused before him, panting.

'You're going to give me that bread, man?' he gasped. 'If I don't get a fix soon, I'm going to blow my cork.'

'Did you find her?'

'Yeah, man, but she's gone. She's with Big Chet. He took her to his pad.'

'Who's Big Chet?'

'Man, he's mean. He runs this freak-out. He's real mean!'

'Where's his pad, Buck?'

'At the far end of the bay. He has a cabin. Give me that hundred, man!'

'How do I know if you're on the beam, Buck. Maybe it's some other girl.'

'I talked with my friends. Big Chet picked this babe off the highway. She calls herself Gina. She's got red hair.'

This satisfied Frost.

'How do I get to the pad, Buck?'

'Right along the beach. It's around half a mile. You can't miss it.'

'Can I get there by car?'

'Sure . . . take the next turning off the highway: brings you right to it.'

Frost gave him the hundred dollar bill.

'Thanks, man,' Buck said, started away, then paused. 'You watch it with Big Chet. Don't tell him who told you,' and he went off in a frantic, shambling run.

Frost hurried back to the Lamborghini. He drove to the highway and took the next turning down to the beach. He turned off the car's headlights and the engine, and coasted down the narrow, sandy track until he was in sight of the sea again.

Leaving the car he walked the next hundred yards. To his left he could see the camp fires. To his right, he saw a small wooden cabin, half hidden under the shade of palm trees. The dim light of an oil lamp showed in a window.

Drawing his gun, he moved silently across the sand until he reached the cabin.

The only sound that came to him was distant guitar music, distant voices and the sea breaking on the beach.

Edging forward, he looked into the lighted room. What he saw there, made him stiffen.

Gina, naked, sat in a broken down armchair. Her hands rested on her knees. There were bloodstains on her hands and on her thighs. Her eyes were blank. She looked like a horrifying wax-work, but he could see by the uneven rise and fall of her breasts, she was alive.

Lit by the smoking oil lamp was the prone figure of a big man, sprawled in death at Gina's feet. He was wearing a grimy sweatshirt and tattered jeans.

Growing out of his chest was the handle of a knife.

Eight

Gun in hand, Frost moved cautiously into the cabin.

The thick smell of dirt, bodies and marihuana smoke was stomach turning. He bent over the body. He guessed this was Big Chet: no longer mean, and as dead as a floater, hauled in from the sea.

The knife had been driven in with such violence, the blade had sealed the wound. There was little bleeding, but the handle of the knife showed blood.

Frost then turned to Gina who sat motionless, her big eyes wide and fixed, her breasts moving as she breathed in spasms.

'Gina!'

No response.

He passed his hand before her eyes, but they remained fixed. He touched her shoulder . . . hot and dry.

One hell of a situation, he thought, and his cop trained mind went into immediate action. What to do? This was murder!

He looked around the squalid cabin. A battered looking telephone stood on a pile of much thumbed *Playboy* magazines. He knew he couldn't handle this situation alone.

He called the Ace of Spades. When Umney came on the line, Frost said, 'I've found her, but there's real trouble. Silk and Mitch around?'

'They've just come in. What trouble?'

'I'm down at Paddler's Creek. I want you three here fast!' Frost snapped. 'Bring trenching tools. We have something to bury!'

'What the hell do you mean?' Umney demanded, alarm in his voice.

'You'll see! Get moving. You know Twin Oakes motel?'

'Yeah, but . . . '

'Take the second turning on your left as you come up the highway before Twin Oakes, then come down to the beach. I'll be waiting for you. I want you three here fast, and don't forget the trenching tools!' Frost hung up.

He went over to Gina and stood looking at her. Apart from her breathing, she could be dead. Again he passed his hand before her eyes, again no response.

He went out of the cabin, and stood breathing in the hot humid air, feeling sweat on his face.

As he stood staring at the moonlit beach, he thought of what Grandi had promised. Five million dollars! This was something Silk, Goble and Umney would not know about! But suppose she died? She looked bad enough to die. The crazy little bitch must have gone on a trip. This big, dead slob must have given her L.S.D. She had flipped her lid and had stabbed the bastard.

He returned to the cabin, hunted around and found a filthy rag which he soaked from a trickle of water from a tap. He washed the blood off her thighs and her hands. She remained like a wax work. Then he looked around and found at the end of a dirty, sagging bed, her clothes: jeans, a T-shirt, panties and sandals.

He went to her and dragged her out of the chair. She flopped like a sawdust doll with escaping sawdust, against him. Somehow, he managed to get her into the jeans. Twice she slipped out of his sweating hands and sprawled on the floor. Twice, cursing, he dragged her up, and finally zipped up the jeans. He was now worried sick. She still remained like a wax work. He got the T-shirt on her, then dropped her back into the chair.

By now, hating the feel of her, sickened by the smell in the cabin, he went out into the open.

He was aware he was wasting time. Gina might die on him. There were complications. Suppose Silk wouldn't play? Suppose he drew back on murder? Suppose he wouldn't bury Big Chet?

Frost thought, then he returned to the cabin and using the telephone, he called the Spanish Bay hotel. Within a minute, Grandi came on the line.

'I have real trouble,' Frost said. 'I've found her, but she is way out on a L.S.D. trip. She looks bad . . . really bad.'

'Can you get her to the Paradise Clinic?' Grandi asked, his voice like a fall of gravel, 'or should I get an ambulance?'

'I'll get her there,' Frost said. 'No ambulance. There are other complications.'

'I'll alert the clinic,' Grandi said, 'and I'll be there.' He hung up.

Frost again looked at Gina, again passed his hands before her eyes. No response. Then he heard the sound of a fast approaching car. He ran out of the cabin as the car pulled up. Silk, Umney and Goble spilled out.

'What the hell is going on?' Silk snarled, walking up to Frost.

'Take a look.'

Frost led the three men into the cabin.

'That's the way I found the scene,' he said.

The three men stared at the dead body, then at Gina.

'Did she kill him?' Umney asked in a hushed voice.

'Who else? She's way out on a trip. She could die on us,' Frost said. 'Get this hunk of meat buried.'

'If she's killed him, we have Grandi just where we want him,' Silk said. 'We can still pick up twenty million dollars.'

'But not if she dies,' Frost said. 'Bury this slob!'

Silk thought for a long moment, then turned to Umney and Goble.

'Bury him, but know where he can be dug up. Bury him just as he is, and don't touch the knife. She'll have her prints on the handle. Get moving!'

While Umney and Goble were dragging the dead body

out of the cabin, Silk smiled evilly at Frost.

'This is the big deal,' he said. 'Grandi pays twenty million or we leak it to the cops. We can't lose this time.'

Frost went to Gina, picked her up, like a sawdust doll, and carried her across the hot sand and through the humid heat to the Lamborghini.

Silk followed.

'Keep out of this!' Frost said as he placed the inert Gina in the passenger's seat. 'Stay away!' He slid into the driving seat, gunned the engine, and leaving Silk, he drove fast up the sandy road to the highway.

It took him fifteen minutes of fast driving to reach the Paradise Clinic. He pulled ιp outside the emergency entrance. It took him less than two minutes to get action. Grandi had already switched on his power. An intern and a nurse were waiting; and they whisked Gina's inert body away.

While he stood by the Lamborghini, sweating in the humid heat, Grandi drove up in the Rolls.

Frost went to meet him.

'She's in emergency,' he said. 'She looks bad.'

Grandi stood motionless, glaring at Frost.

'There's a hell of a complication,' Frost went on. 'She picked up with a wayout freak who fed her L.S.D. She went on a bad trip, and she killed him.'

Grandi stood a step back.

'Killed him?' he croaked.

'Yes . . . she stabbed him to death. The hippy is buried. If we have any luck, no one will know about this, but it'll cost you, Grandi. My associates buried him.'

Grandi stared for a long moment at Frost, then he strode through the swing doors of the emergency entrance and out of sight.

Frost drew in a deep breath. He lit a cigarette with a sweating hand. The sound of a car coming to a screeching halt made him look around. Silk got out of the car and came over.

'What gives?' he demanded, planting himself in front of Frost.

'I told you to keep out of this!' Frost said angrily. 'So keep out of it!'

'Use your head!' Silk said. 'We have Grandi where we want him. She killed this creep and we can prove it. You set up the deal. Squeeze him for twenty million! Tell him he pays or his goddamn daughter faces a murder rap!'

Frost stared at this hatchet-faced, professional killer. He had a sudden feeling of revulsion. It came to him that because of his burning desire to be rich, he had let free this crazy girl, and because she had escaped, she had committed murder. His desire for sudden wealth suddenly turned sour, and he felt sick of himself.

Turning, he made for the emergency entrance.

'Hey! Where are you going?' Silk shouted.

Paying no attention, Frost walked up to the reception desk. An elderly woman looked enquiringly at him.

'A message for Mr Grandi,' Frost said.

The magic name brought the woman immediately alert. 'Yes, sir.'

'Tell him I'll be at the villa if he wants me. The name's Frost.'

She wrote on a scratch pad.

'I'll see he gets your message, Mr Frost.'

A thought dropped into Frost's mind.

'How is Mr Amando?' he asked.

The elderly woman's fat face turned sad.

'He died an hour ago. He had a second heart attack.'

'He's lucky,' Frost said, and leaving her, gaping, he went out into the humid heat.

Silk grabbed hold of his arm.

'Get back in there and talk to Grandi!'

Frost set himself, then smashed his right fist against Silk's jaw. He knew there would now be little pleasure, if any, in his life before him, but, at least, as his knuckles slammed against Silk's face, he did have pleasure.

Silk became airborne. He hurtled backwards and crashed down on the tarmac.

Frost got into the Lamborghini and drove fast to Orchid Villa.

*   *   *   *

Grandi sat in a lounging chair in a small room in which there were other chairs, and a table covered with glossy magazines. The air conditioner made the only sound. He had been sitting there for the past two hours, and while he sat, he thought back on his life.

He had been born in a Naples' slum. His father had been killed in a knife fight. He had a strong tie with his mother, and at the age of six, he was selling phony Parker pens to tourists. Later, he sold them obscene postcards. His mother took all his earnings and saved them. They lived on spaghetti and the fruit he stole from the market. When his mother was killed by a drunk driver who didn't stop, Grandi spent three months mourning. He was then entirely on his own. Using the money, his mother had saved for him, he bought a small cabin cruiser and began the smuggling run between Tangiers and Naples, bringing in cigarettes, then later drugs. Money, always carefully saved, accumulated in the bank. At the age of twenty, because of his knowledge of boats, he became friendly with a rich industrialist who was glad to have him around to handle his motor yacht. He told Grandi he was deeply troubled because his daughter had got involved with a lesbian. Grandi offered his help in return for a large sum of money. The industrialist didn't ask questions, but had agreed. Grandi had walked into a de luxe apartment and had strangled the lesbian to death. Now, suddenly rich, Grandi moved to Rome. At the age of thirty-five, he had invested his money so well, he was now out of the danger of the poverty bracket. He cultivated the right people who were impressed by his shrewdness. He invested, saved, re-invested, expanded. He had the golden touch. When he was forty years of age, and already a multimillionaire, he married Maria Vendotti, the daughter of the Italian ambassador to France. This marriage increased his riches, but he was too occupied in turning his money into more money, and finally after sixteen years, his wife killed herself, and Grandi was left with Gina.

As he sat in the small waiting-room, Grandi realised that Gina was the last of a family link, and family links meant everything to him.

Now, because of this bastard, Frost, Gina was slipping away. Grandi's fingers closed into fists.

Then the door opened and a tall, lean man came in.

'Mr Grandi? I am Doctor Vance. About your daughter...'

Grandi sat like a stone man, listening to the quiet voice.

Finally, Dr Vance said, 'I'm sorry, but I want you to know the facts.'

Grandi looked down at his clenched fists.

'You are telling me there is no hope for her?'

'She will live, but ... no ... there is no hope for her ever to be normal again. She has suffered massive brain damage. We can keep her alive on a machine. That's all we can do. She could live for ten years, even longer.'

'Just breathing?' Grandi asked.

'Yes.'

Grandi clenched his fists.

'Then she's better off dead.'

'That's not for me to say, Mr Grandi,' Vance said quietly. 'It is my job to keep her breathing.'

'You are quite sure there is no possible hope of her recovering?' Grandi asked. 'You are quite sure?'

'No hope at all. The brain damage is massive.'

'I want to see her.'

'Of course. She is on the machine now. Come with me.'

He led Grandi down a long corridor, and into a room where two nurses sat at desks with control panels before them.

In the middle of the room was a bed. Gina lay under a

sheet. Wires and tubes ran from her to the machine that kept her alive.

'All right, nurses,' Vance said curtly. 'I'll call you when I want you.'

Ignoring them, Grandi walked to the bed and looked down at his daughter. For the first time since he had lost his wife, he felt over-powering sorrow, but he kept control of himself. He stood motionless, regarding his last and only link with a family life.

He watched the slow rise and fall of Gina's breasts, hidden by the sheet. He stared at the blank mask of her face and her half open, blank eyes.

'She could remain like this for years?' he asked, half aware that only Vance and himself were now in the room, and the nurses had gone.

'Yes.'

'You are quite sure?'

'Yes. There is no hope for her.' Vance walked around the bed and pointed to a red plug. 'That is the connection to the machine. I must now leave you. I have other patients.' He regarded Grandi. 'If she was my daughter, I would pull out this plug and let her die with dignity.'

Grandi rubbed his hand over his sweating face.

'Is that all I have to do?'

'If the plug remains in, she will continue to breathe. If it is pulled out, she will drift painlessly into death. I'll see you are not disturbed. It is your decision.'

He walked out of the room, closing the door behind him.

Grandi pulled up a chair and sat by the bed. For a long time, he regarded her, watching the rise and fall of her breasts, then suddenly, he realised the hopelessness of it all.

'At least, baby,' he said, 'you killed the bastard who fed you the drug. Now I'm going to kill the bastard who set you free, you poor, crazy little daughter of mine. He'll suffer, baby, be sure of that.' Getting to his feet, he bent and kissed her cheek, then walking around the bed, he pulled out the red plug.

He stood at the foot of the bed, his eyes on the rise and fall of her breasts, then after a while, and when the sheet became still, he put his hand against Gina's face, then left the room.

As he walked across the reception lobby, the nurse at the reception desk said, 'Excuse me, Mr Grandi, there's a message for you.'

Grandi paused.

'Mr Frost says he will be at the Orchid Villa if you want him.'

Grandi stared at her, then inclined his head, then walked on into the hot humid night.

As he was opening the door of the Rolls, a voice, out of the darkness, said 'My name is Lu Silk. I work for Mr Radnitz.'

* * *

Back at his cabin in Orchid Villa, Frost had one burning desire: to get the hell out of Paradise City. The whole set-up had turned sour. His dream of owning five million dollars had gone up in smoke. He felt instinctively that Gina would never again be normal, and it gave him a sick feeling, that he had been responsible for freeing her.

He walked around the room, slamming his fists together. How could he have known she was a nut? How was he to have known that Amando was a brain-shrinker?

What a goddamn mess!

Now, he had to look after himself. He dropped into a lounging chair. He took out his wallet and checked on his money. You can't live, you can't move without money! He still had the four thousand dollars he had got for Gina's ring, and another thousand. So, okay, he was worth five thousand dollars. Where to go? He had no transport. Too risky to take the Lamborghini. Grandi could nail him for stealing his car.

He looked at his watch. The time now was 23.15.

Tomorrow, he told himself, was another day. Getting to his feet he took off his jacket and tie, then walking over to the bed, he dropped on to it.

Tomorrow, he told himself, he would hire a car, and drive away. That would be the end of this stupid nightmare. Drive away to where? He was still wondering, still trying to make a plan for his future life, when he drifted off to sleep.

He came awake four hours later, hearing a constant tapping on the cabin door. He became immediately alert. His hand groped for his gun as he swung his legs off the bed. Holding the gun by his side, he walked to the door.

'Who is it?'

'Ross. Sorry to have woken you up, Mike, but there's talking.'

Keeping the gun behind him, Frost slid the bolt, then stepped back.

'Come on in.'

Umney came in, his charming, wide smile in evidence.

Frost kicked the door shut and slid the bolt. He looked at his watch.

'For God's sake! Do you know the time?'

Umney crossed to one of the lounging chairs and sank into it.

'I could do with a drink.'

Frost slid the gun into his hip pocket.

'What do you want?'

'That's a good question,' Umney said. 'No Scotch?'

'Talk!' Frost said. 'What's all this about?'

'I like you, Mike,' Umney said, smiling. 'You are my people. The moment I saw you, I said ... '

'Skip the crap!' Frost barked. 'You like me as I like you! What are you here for?'

Umney made a grimace.

'Don't play so tough, Mike. I'm sticking my neck out coming here. I want to tell you something. I'm being a good friend.'

'Okay, so tell me,' Frost said, 'and cut the good friend out of the script.'

'It's about Lu,' Umney said.

'What about him?'

'A good question. Lu makes his money putting bullets into people, and he's good at it.' Umney made another grimace. 'We all do things for money . . . that's the way the cookie crumbles, but I don't go along with it. That's why I'm here, Mike.'

Frost tensed.

'So . . . go on.'

'This girl . . . Gina . . . died. She was on a machine that would keep her going for years and Grandi pulled out the plug.' Umney shook his head, and his expression was sorrowful. 'I'm glad I didn't have to do it.'

'Cut the crap, Umney!' Frost said, 'and get to it.'

'Well, once she was dead, there was no money, was there?'

'So, okay, there was no money. It was a foul up. So why are you here?'

'Lu is a professional killer,' Umney said. 'He looks around for money. So he and Grandi got together. I felt I should tell you.'

'Tell me . . . what?' Frost said, staring at Umney.

'A good question,' Umney said with his wide smile. 'Well, Grandi and Lu got together. Grandi needs you dead. He has got this bee that if it hadn't been for you, his crazy daughter would still be screwing and swimming and having a ball. So he comes up with a proposition. He has hired Lu to knock you off. Crazy, isn't it? I thought I'd tip you off.' He rubbed his fingernails on his shirt front. 'The money is good . . . two hundred thousand dollars. We were after millions, but I guess two hundred thousand is better than nothing.'

Frost leaned back in his chair.

'Let me get this straight,' he said. 'Grandi has hired Silk to kill me and the pay-off is two hundred thousand . . . right?'

'That's it,' Umney said. 'Liking you as I do, I thought I would tip you off.'

'When does Silk plan to kill me?' Frost asked.

Umney nodded with approval.

'That's also a good question. So you get the photo, Grandi now hates your guts. He wants to prolong the agony. He's that kind of freak. That's why I'm here to tip you off. It'll be the long gun. Lu's in a class of his own with a silenced telescopic rifle. Last year, he did a job just like this. The money wasn't so good, but it was good enough. He didn't put the guy away for six months, but he kept piling on the pressure, and after six months, this guy was a complete wreck. He was a real toughie, just like you, but after six months, never knowing when he would have a hole in his head, he fell apart.' Umney leaned forward, waving his charming smile at Frost. 'Because I liked this guy, as I liked you, I tipped him off. I told him, as I'm telling you, never walk on a lonely street. Never look out of a window. Never answer a knock on your door without checking. Be careful when you get into a car, and be ready to drop on the floor when the windshield shatters. I told him to go to ground, but I also told him, that sooner or later, Lu would find him.'

'And of course, he did,' Frost said.

'That's right.' Umney's voice hardened. 'This guy followed the tips I had given him, but he ran out of guts. He did something stupid. He got a gun and went looking for Lu.' Umney looked sad. 'This guy's wife gave him a good funeral. Lu sent a wreath.' Umney got to his feet. 'Well, if you're not going to give me a drink, I guess I'll go biddy-byes. I just wanted to tip you off. Sooner or later, Lu will get you lined up. He's a professional.'

Frost leaned back in his chair and released an explosion of laughter.

Umney, staring, stiffened.

'Do you imagine all this crap scares me?' Frost asked. 'It's pathetic. If you imagine you can wage a war of nerves on me, you're a bigger jerk than I thought. Now I'll tell you what you say to this one-eyed phony. Tell him he's picked on the wrong guy to scare. I can take care of myself. I've been taking care of myself since I could walk. Tell him from now on, he and I have a war on. I'm a professional too. His nerve could be softer than mine. Tell him he will have to earn his blood money the hard way, and tell him, I'll kill him with pleasure and for nothing.' Frost pointed a finger. 'Take off. The next time I see your face you start praying. Get out!'

The two men stared at each other. Umney felt a sudden empty sensation inside him. The cold, vicious expression on Frost's face sent a chill through him.

'Don't get me wrong, Mike,' he said hurriedly. 'I'm just passing on the message. I told you, I'm your friend. I am keeping out of this. It's between you and Silk.'

'Losing your guts already?' Frost grinned. 'You're in, and so is your pal, Goble. Tell him. When I've fixed you two, I'll fix Silk, but you two go first.' He drew his gun from his hip pocket and aimed it at Umney. 'Piss off! I won't send a wreath to either you or Goble, but tell Silk, I'll send him one. Get out, before I give you a second navel!'

White faced, Umney bolted out of the cabin.

Frost had a built-in instinct for survival. As the door slammed behind Umney, Frost slid out of his chair, reached the light switch and plunged the room into darkness. He then dropped to the floor.

A split second later, the window smashed and he heard the thud of a bullet into the back of his chair.

He lay still.

A warning shot? Beginning of a war of nerves or was this the business?

He waited until he heard a car start up and drive away. He heard the car stop, then start up again.

Could be Umney had picked up Silk. Could be it was a fake, and Silk was still out there in the darkness.

Frost remained on the floor, his mind active. Silk had proved he was the better man with a rifle, but he still had to prove his nerve was better than Frost's.

During the Vietnam war, Frost had learned you don't sit around, waiting to be shot. You took the initiative. You went out into the jungle, and you hid, and you waited for movement, a rustle of leaves, a passing shadow, a stifled cough, then you squeezed the trigger, and there was one sniper less.

Frost felt a surge of excitement run through him. This threat of death was like a shot of adrenalin in his veins.

'Okay, you one-eyed punk, let's see who's the better man,' he said, half aloud.

Getting silently to his feet, he left the cabin by the back door. Storm clouds shrouded the moon, and it was dark. Even if Silk was still out there among the flowering shrubs and the trees, Frost was confident he couldn't see him.

Keeping in the darkest shadows, he ran silently to the guardroom. He heard the dogs snarling and barking and bounding against their wire compound. No one had fed them. They sounded ferocious.

Reaching the guardroom, Frost closed and locked the door, then turned on the light. From the gun rack he took down one of the automatic rifles, checked the magazine, then laid the rifle on the desk. Then he picked up the telephone receiver and called the guard at the entrance of the villa.

'Did my two friends just leave?' he asked, when the guard came on the line.

'Yeah. I've just checked them out. What's going on?' The guard sounded worried. 'Was it okay I let them in?'

'No problem. I'm leaving. Miss Grandi died. You go home.'

'She died. For the love of mike!'

'I'm shutting the place up. You be here tomorrow at 08.00. Marvin will take over.'

'Well, if you say so . . .'

Frost hung up, then picking up the rifle, he walked back to his cabin. He quickly packed his clothes, then carrying the suitcase and the rifle, he walked to where he had parked the Lamborghini. He was uneasy about taking the car, but he had to get away fast. He remembered what he had been taught in the Army: *Always take the initiative. Always strike first.*

There was a light on in the guardhouse, but the barrier was up. He gave a tap on the horn as the guard appeared in the doorway and shouted something to him, but Frost didn't stop.

The clock on the dashboard showed 03.15. He drove fast to the airport. A sleepy-eyed clerk behind the Hertz desk rented him a 200 Mercedes. He drove the car to where he had parked the Lamborghini, transferred the rifle and his suitcase to the boot of the Mercedes, then headed back to the highway. He stopped at the Twin Oakes motel, booked in and shut himself in a small, air-conditioned cabin. He stripped off his clothes, took a shower, then dropped on to the bed.

Tomorrow, he told himself, would begin his own private war: not a war run by generals who couldn't care less how many men died as long as the battle was won. This was going to be his own private war against three men who had started the war, and he didn't intend to die.

* * *

The time was 02.50.

The Ace of Spades was in darkness except for a light from the room over the swimming pool. The clients had gone home. Marcia had returned to the Spanish Bay hotel. The staff had left.

Mitch Goble sat at the table, a flabby hamburger on a plate before him. His eyes felt heavy. He liked his sleep, but he wanted to know how Umney's prepared talk with Frost had gone off. The three had discussed the best way to soften Frost, and it had been Goble's idea of the long gun threat.

As he was cutting a slice off the hamburger, he heard a

car arrive, then he heard pounding feet, and the door jerked open.

Goble felt an unease run through him when he saw Umney's white, scared face.

'Didn't it work?' he asked, knowing what the answer was going to be.

Umney sat down.

'The bastard laughed at me!'

Goble screwed up his eyes.

'Didn't you lay it on the line, Ross? About the other guy, about . . . '

'Lay it on the line!' Umney shouted. 'I gave him the works but he laughed!'

Goble pushed the plate away. The sight of the hamburger suddenly sickened him.

'Lu agreed that was the way . . . '

'I don't give a goddamn what Lu said!' Umney exclaimed. 'I'm telling you, Mitch! We were crazy in the head to get mixed up with Frost! You've always said he could be too smart! Now, I'm telling you he's going to become more than too smart! He says he is coming after us, and he's going to kill us! If you had seen his face when he said that, you'd be in my state! He'll do it! That look on his face! Jesus! I wish to God I hadn't listened to Lu!'

'Where is Lu?' Goble asked.

'In bed and asleep,' Umney snarled. 'We played it the way we agreed. While I talked to Frost, Lu stayed back with the rifle. When I was through, Lu took a shot at Frost. I wish he had killed him! When I told Lu Frost was going to kill me, he told me not to worry. He said Frost was no problem! Imagine! You know, Mitch, there are times when I wish I had never had anything to do with Lu. He's crazy or something!'

'Get a grip on yourself!' Goble snapped. 'Lu's never steered us wrong. We wouldn't be where we are without him.'

'Now where are we?' Umney demanded. 'We've got this bastard gunning for us!'

At this moment the telephone bell rang, making both men start. Goble snatched up the receiver, listened, then talked.

Getting up, Umney poured himself a big shot of Scotch. His nerves were fluttering so badly what Goble was saying made no sense to him.

Goble hung up.

'That was Hi-Fi. I sent him down to the airport in case Frost took off. Hi-Fi says Grandi's Lamborghini is in the car park and Frost hired a Mercedes from Hertz. Frost could be heading for Miami for a New York flight.'

'No! He's coming after us, Mitch! I know it!' Umney banged his clenched fists together. 'We are crazy to keep this light on! He could be out there with a rifle!'

Goble walked up to Umney and hit him across his face.

'Wrap up! We've got to find Frost before he goes into action. Lu has gone to bed. Could be Frost has also gone to bed. So we start checking the motels. I'll take the west side. You the east side. Come on, Ross! How many finks have we set up for Lu? This is just another fink! Get started!'

After half an hour, Goble called the Twin Oakes motel. He had called four other motels, now he struck gold.

'Yes, sir,' a voice told him. 'A man booked in half an hour ago. He had a Mercedes. He is registered in the name of Peter Jarrow.'

'Tall, dark, good looking?'

'That is an exact description, sir,' the voice said, now sounding worried. 'I hope there is no trouble.'

Goble had identified himself as Sergeant Baski of the Paradise City traffic control.

'Routine check,' Goble said. 'No problem,' and he hung up. He was so pleased with his quick success he didn't take into consideration the night clerk's reaction.

As Goble ran to the door and bawled down the passage, 'I've found him!' the night clerk who had lived in Paradise City all his life and was on good terms with the police, slowly replaced the receiver. Sergeant Baski! This was a name unknown to him.

The night clerk who was a seventeen-year-old student, doing night duty to earn a few dollars while he worked for a master's degree in economics, decided that a call from the police about a routine check at 03.50 was more than odd.

He called the police headquarters and asked the night duty sergeant to be connected with Sergeant Baski, traffic control.

The night duty sergeant said in a bored voice, 'You have made a mistake. We don't have any Baski. What's this all about?'

The night clerk hung up.

Two minutes later, the sound of the telephone bell woke Frost. He came awake, alert, and became even more alert as he listened to what the night clerk told him.

'Thanks,' he said. 'I have a drunken friend who starts trouble. Forget it, but thanks all the same.'

Frost slid off the bed.

So they had found him! Silk could be out there in the darkness, waiting for him. Frost groped around in the dark, found the rifle, then dropping flat, he edged open the cabin door and looked out into the night.

The sky had a purple light. The palms and the shrubs were sharp edged against the coming dawn. In another ten minutes, it would be dangerously light.

Frost felt completely relaxed. This was the kind of warfare he revelled in. Moving like a silent snake, pulling the rifle with him, he crawled into the open.

Nothing happened. Nothing moved.

He decided it was too soon for Silk to take action, but he took no chances. He reached the Mercedes as the edge of the sun came up behind the trees. With one swift movement, he had the car door open and slid in, ducking down, he waited. His built-in instinct showed him the green light.

He started the car and drove fast towards the Ace of Spades.

* * *

Silk lifted his head off the pillow and glared with his one eye at Umney who stood in the doorway.

'Can't you see I'm trying to sleep!' he snarled.

Umney moved into the room, snapping on the light.

'Frost is at the Twin Oakes motel,' he said excitedly. 'You can take him!'

'Get the hell out of here,' Silk barked. 'I'm trying to sleep!'

'Lu . . . for God's sake! Frost is dangerous!' Umney came to stand at the foot of the bed. 'This is the time to fix him!'

Silk rolled on to his back and yawned.

'I made a deal with Grandi and I stay with it,' he said. 'We are going to break Frost's nerve. What's the matter with you? You want a piece of the money, don't you? We rush this and Grandi won't pay. Leave me sleep!'

'All you have to do, Lu, is go to the Twin Oakes motel and nail him!' Umney said. 'If you don't nail him now, he's going to nail us!'

'Get the motel staked out,' Silk said. 'We wait. I can take care of Frost any day. Turn that goddamn light out. I want some sleep!'

With a sick feeling of fear and frustration, Umney turned off the light and returned to the room over the swimming pool.

'He's crazy!' he said, his voice shaking. 'He says to stake out the motel and when he's ready, he'll take care of Frost. He says Grandi won't pay unless it's slow! Jesus! While we're farting around, Frost could come after us!'

Goble had just finished the hamburger.

'Take it easy, Ross. No need to get excited. I've alerted Louie to watch the motel. He'll be there in twenty minutes. Frost won't do anything. He's not all that stupid. If Lu

177

wants it slow, we do what he wants. He's never been wrong, so quit yelling.' He got to his feet. 'I'm going to bed. Look at the goddamn time.' He walked over to the window and drew back the curtains. 'Look, the sun's coming up.'

He presented an irresistible target to Frost, hidden by the flowering shrubs. Frost lifted the rifle, aimed and gently squeezed the trigger.

The top of Goble's head exploded, scattering brains and blood, and he went down like a stricken elephant, taking with him the table and two chairs.

For a brief paralysed moment, Umney stared, then threw himself on the floor as another bullet smashed the screen of the big TV set by which he was standing.

Umney, his heart hammering, sweat pouring down his face, lay still. To his horror, he found his hands were lying in Goble's blood.

Hearing the two rifle shots and the thud of Goble's body as it hit the floor, Silk swung off the bed, slid into a black shirt and black trousers and into sandals. His movements were fast but unflustered. He snatched up the target rifle, crossed the room in two swift strides and stuffed a .38 automatic into his hip pocket, then he opened the door and stepped out into the half dark corridor.

His thin lips were drawn back in a snarl of fury.

'Ross! Mitch!'

He started down the corridor, then paused as he saw Umney come crawling out of the room above the swimming pool. Umney was making a gibbering noise of fear.

The sun was now above the trees and there was enough light for Silk to see Umney's bloodstained hands. He moved by Umney and peered into the room.

A beam of sunlight fell directly on Goble. One quick look told Silk all he wanted to know. He reached forward and pulled the door shut, then putting down the rifle, he caught hold of Umney by his shirt and dragged him upright.

'I told you! I warned you!' Umney said hysterically.

'He's out there! He's going to kill us both!'

Silk slammed him hard against the wall, shook him and then slapped his face.

'He's not going to kill you and he's not going to kill me!' Silk bit off the words. 'Mitch was unlucky, but not us. Okay, so he's out there. He's on our ground! We'll take him!'

Shaking, Umney stared at Silk.

'He's killed Mitch!' he cried. 'He's out there! If we show ourselves, he'll shoot us! You said you could take care of him, and now look what's happened!'

Scarcely listening, Silk's mind was busy. The whole operation had been an utter foul-up, but, at least, out of the mess, he had got Grandi's promise to pay two hundred thousand dollars to kill Frost, but the agreement had been to make Frost sweat, and not to hurry the killing. Silk realised now he had greatly underestimated Frost. He should have listened to Umney's warning that Frost wasn't going to be scared. Frost had had the nerve to come out here and kill Mitch. The chances were that Frost was still out there, rifle in hand. Silk was very confident in his own shooting. If Frost was out there, then he was as good as dead. Silk was determined to earn the promised money, but he wasn't going to take any chances unless he was sure of getting the money.

'Stay right here,' he said to Umney, and he moved swiftly to the office. The curtains were drawn but, taking no chances, Silk snatched up the telephone, sat on the floor, away from the window, and called the Spanish Bay hotel.

The time now was 04.55.

At first the night reception clerk refused to connect Silk with Grandi's suite at such an hour, but when Silk said there was an emergency, he did so.

Grandi's voice came on the line. Silk was surprised how alert Grandi sounded, but he wasn't to know Grandi had been sitting by the window all night, mourning for his daughter.

Speaking softly, Silk explained the situation.

'There are two things I can do, Mr Grandi,' he concluded. 'It's for you to decide. Frost has killed my partner. I can call the police and they'll take over and arrest Frost. He'll talk. The newspapers will headline your daughter. The best solution would be for me to fix him right now if he is out there, and I think he is. But before I go hunting for him, I want to know I get paid. What's it to be?'

'Kill him now and you'll get paid,' Grandi said, a snarl in his voice, and he hung up.

For a minute or so, Silk remained on the floor, his evil smile in evidence. He thought, then nodding, he got up and joined Umney who was leaning against the wall of the corridor, his face ashen as he breathed in frightened gasps.

'Grandi says take him now,' Silk said. 'So, we take him.'

Umney stared at Silk, horror in his eyes.

'Not me!' he quavered. 'This is your end of the pitch! I'm staying right here!'

'He may have gone,' Silk said, 'but we've got to find out. Now you are going through the door, Ross, with your hands on your head and you're going to yell I'm not here and not to shoot. Then when he shows himself, I'll take him.'

'You're crazy! The moment I show myself, he'll kill me!' Umney began trembling.

'No, he won't. He wants me. Come on, Ross, get going!'

'No! You can't do this to me, Lu! I'm not going! I'm not going to walk out there to be killed!'

Silk transferred the rifle to his left hand and jerked out the .38. He held the barrel within inches of Umney's sweating face.

'Make up your goddamn mind!' he snarled, his face a mask of vicious fury. 'If you don't get moving in ten seconds, I'll blow your head off!'

Umney sucked in his breath with a sob.

The look in the one glittering eye told him he was within seconds of death.

'Okay . . . okay . . . I'll go.'

Silk stepped back.

'Take it dead slow. Start shouting as soon as you open the door. He won't kill you, but I'll nail him. Get going!'

Umney stumbled down the corridor to the door leading into the garden. Silk shoved the .38 into his hip pocket, then moved silently after Umney, the rifle now in both hands.

Umney looked beseechingly at him as his hand fumbled for the door handle.

'Yell loud!' Silk said, 'and hurry it up! He may have gone.'

*　*　*

As Frost saw Goble reel back, blood on his face, then drop out of sight, he felt a surge of elation run through him. He saw a movement of white through the window and immediately fired again. He heard the smash of glass as the TV tube exploded.

Then moving swiftly, crouched down, keeping under cover of the flowering shrubs he changed his position some fifty yards further away.

He paused and flattened out, knowing he was completely concealed. He wondered if he had killed Umney. He thought not, but with luck he could have winged him, but he must still count two against one.

He lay there, listening, but heard nothing. He was able to survey the whole front of the restaurant. There was no cover. If either Silk or Umney came out through the front entrance, they would be committing suicide. There was probably a side or a back door. He wanted them penned up in the restaurant. Once they were in the open they could split up, and that would shorten the odds in their favour.

Moving silently, still behind the screen of shrubs, Frost surveyed the left side of the restaurant and saw a door at

181

the head of a short flight of wooden stairs. He kept moving, and around the back of the restaurant he saw the staff entrance. This was bare of cover. He decided if they were coming out they would use the side door. He moved back until he was some sixty yards from the side door. He was in a perfect position: complete cover, yet with a clear field of fire. He settled down to wait.

By now the sun had come up behind the trees, casting lean shadows. Frost looked at his watch. The time was close on 05.00. He wondered at what time the staff would arrive. If Silk and Umney elected to stay put, under cover, he would have a problem, but he doubted if they would. They would have to get Goble's body out of sight. Silk wouldn't want to get involved with the police. Silk had to try to kill him before the staff arrived.

A half hour crept by, but Frost was used to waiting. He remembered he had waited four long hours in the jungle for a sniper to show. He relaxed, the rifle at his shoulder, aimed at the door and waited.

There was no sound except the distant traffic, no movement except a hawk floating in the sky.

Then the side door opened and Umney stood in the doorway, his hands clasped on top of his head.

It would be a difficult shot, Frost thought. The angle was wrong. He couldn't risk a miss.

Umney screamed, 'Don't shoot! Lu's not here! I'll help you find him! Don't shoot!'

Frost's mind flashed back into the past. He was once faced with exactly the same situation. He had cornered a Viet sniper who had yelled to him that he surrendered. From out of the thicket where he was hiding, the sniper had thrown his rifle which had landed near Frost. Then the sniper had appeared, his hands in the air, and Frost had fallen for it. He came out of his hide, his rifle level. The sniper took off his conical straw hat in which was concealed a hand grenade. As Frost shot him, the hat floated towards him. For a split second, Frost had watched death floating towards him, then he dropped flat. He had spent two months in a field hospital with splinter wounds, but he had survived. He had promised himself that if ever a man came towards him with his hands in the air, he would shoot first, and apologise later.

He rose up on one knee to correct the angle of fire.

Silk lying on the floor of the corridor, peering through the open doorway, caught the movement, but Umney was in the way.

Umney was yelling at the top of his voice. Silk didn't dare shout to him to drop so he could nail Frost. He didn't want Frost to know he was there.

Frost shot Umney through the head as he reached the bottom step, then Frost dropped flat, but he wasn't quick enough.

As Umney was falling, Silk got a clear line of fire and squeezed off a shot. The bullet went through Frost's ribs and his arm, ploughing a furrow through the flesh of Frost's chest. He glimpsed Silk, scrambled back, out of sight. He fired. The bullet whistled by Silk's face and sent wood splinters flying. One big splinter smashed Silk's glass eye, bringing blood running down his face. Cursing, Silk retreated further down the corridor.

Frost, feeling blood soaking his shirt, crawled away. His Army training stood him in good stead, and like a snake, silent and not moving the shrubs, he reached a clump of trees away from the side door without drawing any more fire.

He looked at his bloodstained shirt, flexed his fingers, grimaced and told himself it could have been worse.

How that one-eyed bastard could shoot! he thought. Well, it's between the two of us now. One against one . . . fair enough. Silk's expertise with a rifle against his expertise as a jungle fighter. It bothered him that he was bleeding, but he had bled before. He took out his handkerchief, made it into a pad and, using his belt, strapped the pad against the wound. Then he crawled away to another position where he had a clear view of the side door, and he settled down to wait.

Silk went quickly down the corridor, down the stairs to the toilets. He bathed his face and stopped the bleeding: a mere scratch. He wasn't sure if he had hit Frost. If not hit, was Frost still covering the side door? Silk looked at his watch. Time was running out. In another hour the staff would be arriving. He had to kill Frost quickly, then he would fade out of the scene. He had good contacts who would give him a cast iron alibi. The police wouldn't be able to pin any of these killings on him, but Frost had to be killed or if arrested, he would talk.

Maybe he was already dead, Silk thought, but he mustn't take any chances. He was now sure he was within grasping distance of two hundred thousand dollars. What to do? If Frost were only winged, he would be as dangerous as a cornered tiger, and he was concealed.

Certainly too dangerous to leave the building by the side door. There was no cover from the main entrance nor from the staff entrance.

The roof!

Silk cursed under his breath. Why hadn't he thought of the roof before. If he had gone up there when Umney had made his exit, Frost would be dead by now.

Catching up his rifle, he ran up the stairs and to the fire exit. He climbed the iron ladder that brought him on to the flat roof around which was a two foot high wall.

Dropping flat, Silk crawled across the roof until he was immediately above the side door, some ten feet below.

Frost, lying amongst the shrubs saw there was a small puddle of blood beside him. He looked at the pad which was soaked and he began to feel uneasy.

'Jesus!' he thought. 'I'm bleeding like a goddamn pig!'

Savagely, he tightened the belt, holding the pad, and pain shot through him. He was aware of lassitude, and the rays of the sun beating down on him, bothered him. He was also developing a raging thirst.

You one-eyed bastard, he thought. You've really done damage! Well, come on, damn you . . . show yourself!

All was silence and stillness except for the hawk, still floating in the sky.

Frost thought of Marcia. Out of the past, he heard her say, *Paradise City is where the real action is. There's more money to be picked up there than in any other city in the world.*

How he wished he hadn't listened to her!

A dream of five million dollars! Some dream!

If he got out of this mess alive, what would he do? Once more hunting for the crock of gold: always in sight, but always out of reach! That had been his life, and would be his future life.

There was a relaxed feeling of lightness in his body that urged him to sleep. The pool of blood around him was growing larger. He shook his head, blinked his eyes and caught hold of the rifle.

Dismay ran through him as he found the rifle impossibly heavy.

'I'm bleeding to death,' he said, half aloud. He made a clumsy effort and dragged up the rifle, disturbing the shrubs around him.

Watching from above, Silk saw the movement, then he saw Frost. His thin lips drew back in a snarl. In one swift movement, he aimed his rifle and fired.

At that moment, Frost looked up and saw Silk on the roof. His reflexes had gone. He saw the gun, but there was nothing he could do. He knew he was an instant away from death. His last thought, as he died, was that this one-eyed punk had beaten him.

Silk knew he didn't have to fire again. He stood up, stretched, then walked to the edge of the parapet. He looked down at the still body.

Two hundred thousand dollars! Well, no one could say he hadn't earned it. This had been the most dangerous and tricky kill of his long list of killings.

Then he heard what sounded like the whirring of wings. A bird?

As he began to look around, the blade of a throwing

knife buried itself in his back. In agony, he crouched forward, lost his balance and fell the twenty feet on to the grass, writhed, then went still.

Suka, dressed in black, climbed down the iron ladder, ran out of the restaurant and paused beside Silk. He kicked him over, pulled out the knife, wiped the blade on Silk's shirt, then walked to where Umney was lying. Satisfied that he too was dead, he walked over to Frost. He looked down at his body for a few moments, nodded, then ran swiftly into the thickets from whence he had come.

* * *

Grandi was speaking to Dr Vance over the telephone.

'I want my daughter's body sent to Rome, doctor,' he was saying. 'I will leave the arrangements to you. Rome was her city.'

'Yes, Mr Grandi. I will arrange everything.'

'Thank you.' A pause. 'I will see that your hospital is endowed,' and Grandi hung up.

He heard a slight sound behind him. He looked around. Suka had come in and was standing by the door.

'All dead, signor,' he said, as if announcing dinner was served.

'Silk?'

'All dead as you instructed.'

Grandi thought of his daughter.

'Pack,' he said. 'We leave for Rome in an hour.'

'Yes, signor.'

Grandi moved to the big, picture window and looked down at the bay. In spite of the early hour, yachts, with their multi-coloured sails were already leaving the harbour. Already people were coming down to the beach. The traffic was building up. The hot breeze was moving the heads of the palm trees.

Paradise City was beginning yet another day.

THE END

›› If you've enjoyed this book and would like to discover more great vintage crime and thriller titles, as well as the most exciting crime and thriller authors writing today, visit: ›››

The Murder Room
Where Criminal Minds Meet

themurderroom.com